Climbing to the top of the world...

"Are you ready?" Kallyn shouldered a small backpack and popped open her umbrella.

Cece looked up at the Wall. "Yeah, I'm ready."

Kallyn and Cece steadily made the climb.

The steps became much steeper, and the path narrowed. Higher and higher they climbed, the gap between them and the rest of the students widening. Cece caught her breath and looked up, unable to see where the stairs ended.

"Just think how good you'll feel when we make it to the top, Cece," Kallyn said.

Just how good will *it feel when I get to the top?* Cece thought. By far, this was one of the hardest things she had ever done. If she could climb to the highest point of this section of the Great Wall, she could do anything. Tomorrow's trip to the orphanage would seem like nothing.

"We're almost there," Kallyn said.

Cece looked up again. She could do this. She *had* to do this.

Finally, Cece was only steps from the last tower. She had just five steps left. *Four...* Her body filled with anticipation. *Three... two...*

She took the last step, and relief washed over her. Cece looked all around her. She felt like she was literally on top of the world.

The Great Call of China

Cynthea Liu

speak

An Imprint of Penguin Group (USA) Inc.

Acknowledgments

I wish to acknowledge my rockstar agent Jen, my tireless and smarty editor Karen, and my critique partner Tam, otherwise known as America's Next Top Model. A special thanks goes to my big brother William, my Xi'an connection and resident expert. Oh, yeah. And he's good looking, too.

SPEAK
Published by the Penguin Group
Penguin Group (USA) Inc.,
345 Hudson Street, New York, New York 10014, U.S.A.
Penguin Group (Canada), 90 Eglinton Avenue East, Suite 700, Toronto, Ontario, Canada M4P 2Y3
(a division of Pearson Penguin Canada Inc.)
Penguin Books Ltd, 80 Strand, London WC2R 0RL, England
Penguin Ireland, 25 St Stephen's Green, Dublin 2, Ireland (a division of Penguin Books Ltd)
Penguin Group (Australia), 250 Camberwell Road, Camberwell, Victoria 3124, Australia
(a division of Pearson Australia Group Pty Ltd)
Penguin Books India Pvt Ltd, 11 Community Centre, Panchsheel Park, New Delhi - 110 017, India
Penguin Group (NZ), 67 Apollo Drive, Rosedale, North Shore 0632, New Zealand
(a division of Pearson New Zealand Ltd)
Penguin Books (South Africa) (Pty) Ltd, 24 Sturdee Avenue, Rosebank, Johannesburg 2196,
South Africa

Registered Offices: Penguin Books Ltd, 80 Strand, London WC2R 0RL, England

Published by Speak, an imprint of Penguin Group (USA) Inc., 2008

1 3 5 7 9 10 8 6 4 2

Copyright © Cynthea Liu, 2009

CIP DATA IS AVAILABLE.

SPEAK ISBN 978-0-14-241134-6 (pbk.)

Printed in the United States of America

For my daughter Clara. Live strong.

Cece's Xi'an

Muslim Quarter

Application for the Students Across the Seven Seas
Study Abroad Program

Name: Celise "Cece" Charles

Age: 16

High School: Lamar High

Hometown: Dallas, Texas

Preferred Study Abroad Destination: Xi'an, China, Anthropology Program

1. Why are you interested in traveling abroad next year?

Answer: Visiting a real dig—especially one as rich as Xi'an's Terra Cotta Warriors—is an opportunity I can't miss. Also, going to China will give me the chance to explore my roots.

(Truth: I'm so tired of my ho-hum high school, my boring job, and my mom, who hates the idea of me going to China. She's afraid I'll go looking for my birth parents. Which is exactly what I intend to do, hence the "exploring my roots" part.)

2. How will studying abroad further develop your talents and interests?

Answer: The skills I gain from learning about Chinese culture will be invaluable to my future career in anthropology.

(Truth: Going to China will be invaluable to my sanity. I can't spend another summer working as a parking-lot attendant for Six Flags.)

3. Describe your extracurricular activities.

Answer: National Honor Society, Academic Decathlon, Whiz Quiz team, Student Council treasurer.

(Truth: Sigh. That is the truth.)

4. Is there anything else you feel we should know about you?

Answer: I love learning about people who lived long ago, the languages they spoke, and their struggles. I believe the insight we gain from the past can prepare us for the future, and I am excited to share my enthusiasm for this field with other like-minded students.

(Truth: What I want most of all is some answers to my own past. I also need some fun and excitement in my life. Though Alison, my best friend, says I just need a guy. So maybe that, too.)

Chapter One

Cece and Alison flipped through a pile of jeans at Macy's. Cece was looking for a pair to replace her worn-out boot-cuts. She needed something new and fresh for her trip to China.

Alison held up a pair. "Size four, right?"

"Perfect," Cece said, taking the jeans. It was the last item on her list, and the mall would be closed soon. "I'll try these on and then we'll be done."

Cece headed for the fitting rooms with Alison trailing behind. "I can't believe you're leaving me tomorrow," Al said.

"How am I going to survive the summer without you?"

Cece walked into an open fitting room and closed the door while Al waited outside. "Beats me." Cece hung up the jeans and her purse. "I guess you and Eugene Derkle will have to keep each other company." She grinned, then tugged off her skirt and put on the jeans. She was thrilled to spend a summer without Eugene, her manager at Six Flags. He was the kind of guy you caught picking his nose. Like all the time.

"Don't remind me," Alison said. "His knee socks will be the end of me. Are you sure you have to go?"

Cece zipped up the jeans and observed herself in the mirror. *Not bad.* The slim cut made her look even taller. "Yes, I'm sure. The S.A.S.S. anthropology program is great. I'm really excited about it." That, and there was no way she was going to suffer another tourist season in Texas, stuffed inside a hot toll booth. She turned and looked over her shoulder to check the rear view. The jeans made her butt look round, perky even. *Excellent.*

"What about your mother?" Alison's voice filled with hope. "Is she having second thoughts? Maybe canceled your plane tickets?"

"Ha, you wish." Cece turned and checked the front again. "But I do think she wants to plant a tracking device under my skin before I go. Do you know how many times she's told me to be sure to e-mail? To not forget my calling card? Blah, blah, blah…"

Lately, Mom's smothering problem had gotten worse, as if that was even possible. It wasn't like Cece was going to be gone forever. It was just *one* summer, halfway around the globe. *No big deal.*

"You know why she's worried, right?" Al's voice got low. "It's not like she doesn't know about your special plans."

Cece opened the door.

Al was leaning against the wall. "Hey, those jeans look awesome."

Cece pulled her in and shut the door. "Wait a second. How do you know she knows?"

Al frowned. "*Please.* Don't all moms figure out stuff like that? She's got to have some idea you're not going to China just to traipse around ancient ruins and study fossils."

"Artifacts," Cece corrected as she tugged off her jeans. "Okay, so let's say she does know. She's not stopping me. Maybe she's finally all right with me learning more about my birth parents." She grabbed her skirt and put it on. "I mean, I'm about to turn seventeen. I'm practically an adult."

Al stared at Cece. "This *is* your mom you're talking about."

Cece raised an eyebrow. "True." So maybe that was wishful thinking. She straightened her skirt in the mirror. More than likely, her mother was putting up a good front instead. Perhaps the reason she hadn't stopped her was

because Cece had played the old "but how can you prevent me from furthering my education?" card. If there was one thing Mom couldn't do, it was jeopardize her education. Plus, Dad was 100 percent behind the trip. When Cece had brought up the program to her parents, her father said he thought they should let Cece broaden her experience and get to know her birth country. Mom had no choice but to cave. "Well, if she does know," Cece said, picking up the jeans from the floor, "I'll just have to be extra careful then. You'll help cover for me, right?"

"Sure," Al replied. "I want you to find what you're looking for just as much as you do, but don't make me lie too much. If your mom asks me point-blank, 'Is Cece visiting the orphanage in Beijing?' I don't think I can pull it off. I like your mom. She's sweet."

Cece slung the jeans over her arm. "I know, I know." She prayed her mother wouldn't have the guts to ask Alison something like that. She grabbed her purse. "Any last words of wisdom?"

Alison got up. "As a matter of fact, there are. Do something *fun* while you're there, okay?" She opened the door.

"I'll try." Cece said, following Alison out. "That's the other reason I'm going. I haven't forgotten."

They headed for the registers.

"By fun, I don't mean studying, Cece."

"I know that."

"Then there's only one more thing."

Cece let out a breath. "What now?"

"Make sure you give yourself something extra special for your birthday. You know, because it'll be the first time since forever that I won't be there to celebrate."

Cece paused. She hadn't even thought about that. Her seventeenth birthday would fall just before the program ended. It wouldn't be the same without her best friend. She sighed. "Something special, huh? Like what?"

"Oh...I don't know...." Al stopped by an accessory counter and browsed through one of the racks. "Since you're sure to meet some guys over there, you should be totally open to all the possibilities." She stopped to smile at Cece. "You should give yourself *the gift of love*."

Cece rolled her eyes. "Which talk show did you get that from?"

"I didn't get it from a show," Al said. She spun the rack. "I read it in a book. It's great advice. This summer is the perfect opportunity to break the man drought you're in."

"Man drought?" Cece said in surprise. "I'd hardly call it that. I attract plenty of men. Just not the right ones." Last month, it had been some high school dropout from work. A couple of months before, a guy on her academic team who had a bad case of halitosis. And before that? One of her mother's friend's sons—his idea of a date was going to the library.

"All I'm saying is to keep an eye out," Al said. "Someone there just might be worthy." She pulled a pair of earrings off the rack.

"Look, Al, if the right guy comes along, you know I'm all over that."

"You mean *him,* right?"

Cece laughed. "No comment."

"Well, maybe you'll want to get these." Al passed a pair of red rose-shaped earrings to Cece. "If any earrings say romance, these are it."

Cece held the jewelry up to her ear and looked at herself in the mirror. The earrings brought out the pink in her cheeks and lips. "Sold."

After Cece made her purchases, she and Alison walked out of the store. Cece glanced at her watch and took in a huge breath. She had only twelve hours left before she'd be on a plane to China. "This is it. You parked on the other side of the mall, right?"

"Yeah," Al said. "I guess it's time to say good-bye."

"Yup."

"Time to leave your friend thousands and thousands of miles behind."

"Yup."

"Time to—"

"Al, stop. You can always e-mail me. It'll be like I never left."

"All right, chica." Alison gave Cece a hug. "I'll try not to get too sad while I rot at Six Flags, with Eugene, in one-hundred-degree weather..."

"Oh, shut up!" Cece laughed as she broke apart from Al. "You'll be fine. Now go."

"Okay," Alison said grudgingly. She started to walk away, then gave Cece one last wave. "Bye!"

Cece waved back. "Bye."

She smiled before she turned for the exit. She'd really miss Alison.

When Cece got home, she went to her room to finish packing. She took her new jeans from the bag and put them on top of the rest of the clothes in her suitcase. Then she picked up some frames from her nightstand and slipped out the photos—one of her parents taken on their twentieth anniversary and one of Al and her on a roller coaster, arms up, screaming. That was when they'd thought working at an amusement park would be fun.

Someone knocked at the door.

"Yeah?" Cece said.

Cece's mother, Sheryl, poked her head in. "I thought I heard you come home. I almost forgot to give you this." She stepped in and dangled a shiny cell phone from her fingertips. "The cell phone company says it'll work in China. But it's two dollars a minute, so emergencies only?" She held out a bright yellow bag. "I got the travel charger, too."

Cece took the bag from her mother. "But you already gave me a calling card."

Her mother crossed her arms. "A calling card won't do any good if you're trapped in a pit somewhere, will it?"

Cece smiled. *She had a point; you never know when you're going to be trapped in a pit.* She put the phone and the charger into her backpack. "Thanks. Anything else?"

"No, I think that's it." But her mother didn't move from her spot. Instead, she looked at her daughter like she was doing a mental inventory of every inch of her face—right down to the tiny birthmark on her cheek.

"Um…Mom…you're staring."

"Sorry, honey. I just wonder what this summer will be like without you."

Oh, man. Maybe her mother and Alison could form a support group together.

"Don't forget what I said the other night, okay? Xi'an isn't like our quiet little neighborhood. Don't walk alone, watch for pickpockets, and keep that cell with you—"

"*Mom,* I'll be fine," Cece said, giving her a hug.

"You sure?"

"Yes." Cece rested her chin on her mother's shoulder, and she could practically feel her mom's worry. Cece filled with guilt when she thought of her plans for visiting the orphanage, but she wouldn't change her mind now. She had to know more about her birth parents; China was calling to her.

Her mother held her tighter.

Just then, her father walked in. "Sheryl, the girl is leaving no matter how hard you hug her."

Sheryl finally let Cece go. "I know, Ed."

"C, I'll be taking you to the airport," her dad said. "Your mother has to work at the hospital in the morning."

"I really wish I could go along," Sheryl added.

"That's okay," Cece said. "I'll say good-bye to you before I go."

"Okay, honey."

"Now try to get some sleep," Ed said. "Let's go, Sheryl." He steered her toward the door. "Cece's got a big day tomorrow."

After her parents left, Cece closed her door and leaned against it for a moment. Then she went to her bed. There was one more thing she needed to pack. She lifted the dust ruffle and retrieved a sweater box that contained her old school papers. She dug to the bottom and pulled out another picture. This one was small, a little aged at the edges. It had been taken on the day Cece's parents came to China to adopt her.

Cece looked at the two-year-old toddler in the photograph, standing between her new parents on a cobblestone walk. Her hair was stick straight and bowl cut, and she wore a light jacket with a mandarin collar, and cloth shoes. With one hand, she held her mother's hand and in the other, an ice-cream pop that looked like a Dove bar.

Behind them, Asian people crowded the streets.

It was hard for Cece to believe that innocent-look-ing child in a foreign land was the same jeans-wearing, pop-music-loving, American teen she was today. Only a couple of things remained the same; she still had the heart-shaped face and the beauty mark on her cheek. But gone was the chubbiness of her toddler arms and legs. In their place was a thin girl, with side-swept bangs and long, smooth hair, who wondered if she had her mother's lanky stature or her father's piercing brown eyes.

And there was one more thing that hadn't change. She still loved ice-cream pops. Her father had joked it took only an ice-cream treat to get Cece to leave the country quietly with two strangers. Cece grinned, then flipped the photo over to where she had copied the address of the orphanage. Only a few days before, she had met her dad for coffee at a diner near their house. Over the years, the diner had become their place for serious father-daughter talks, since it was hard to have any real privacy at home with Mom around. When Cece had walked in, she had mentally prepared for a lecture—on what, she wasn't sure. But as she sat down, he reached into his shirt pocket and scooted a piece of paper across the table. "C, I'd rather you go to the right place than poke your nose in all the wrong ones," he'd said.

Cece looked at the paper. He had written an address on it. "Dad—"

He put his hand up.

"Don't say a word, Cece. I know Mom would never agree with what I'm doing, but I think you ought to see the orphanage where you spent your first two years."

As Cece stared at the address, guilt washed over her. She didn't want to admit she'd already raided the family safe weeks ago and had found the address on her adoption papers. She quickly tucked the note into her purse. She knew she'd have to keep this between the two of them. Since Cece could remember, her mother had never been comfortable with questions about Cece's adoption and her birth parents. "Cece," she would say, "can it just be okay to know that we're your family?"

Cece believed her mother must have felt threatened by the possibility of Cece finding her biological parents. Maybe she didn't want to share the bond they had with someone else. Or maybe she worried Cece might replace her altogether. Of course, that last one was ridiculous. Cece couldn't imagine having anyone else as her mom, but she didn't blame her for feeling insecure. She only wished her mother understood how much she loved her.

Cece's father, on the other hand, had always been more sympathetic, and he actually had been able to convince her mother to open up once about the adoption. When Cece was twelve, they both sat down with her and stated plainly they didn't know anything about her birth parents, but they'd tell her everything they knew. They described the orphanage, told her what her name used to be before

her adoption—Bei Ma Hua—and they showed her some photos, including the one Cece now kept with her.

After her parents had finished, Cece had only one question, and it was big. "Why do you think my birth parents let me go?"

Her parents had looked uncomfortable, and an awkward silence fell over the room. Finally, her father spoke. "Cece, I can't speak for your birth parents, but I can make some guesses...." He said her mother could have gotten pregnant out of wedlock and been unable to raise her alone. Or maybe her parents were poor and couldn't afford to keep her. Or... "China also has something called a one-child policy," her father had said. He went on to explain that the policy was created to prevent overpopulation—a law that allowed each couple to have only one child. As a result, many families wanted a boy so he could carry on the family name. So if a couple had a girl first, sometimes that girl would be abandoned, allowing the couple to try again for a son.

It took a few seconds for the information to soak in. What was her dad saying? *My parents left me because I'm a girl?*

"Mom," Cece had said, "do you believe that's what happened?"

She nodded reluctantly. "It's certainly possible."

That night, Cece went to bed a different person. Older, somehow, completely wrapped up in a tangled ball of emotions. A part of her was confused, disappointed, even angry. And a very small part, from deep within her heart, refused to believe it. Could her birth parents leave her simply because she was a girl? She didn't think so. Or at least she didn't *want* to think so. It was this part of her that got her to sleep that night as she held the picture of herself in China. And it was this part of her that had gotten her to sleep every night for a long time.

After her father had handed Cece the note, he leaned back in the booth. It was as though he wasn't sure of what he'd just done. At last, he said, "If you contact the orphanage, have no expectations, all right?"

Cece nodded, and her father looked satisfied.

Now Cece stared at the address on the back of the photo, as if it held the answer to all her questions. "No expectations," she whispered.

But as she slipped the photo into her wallet, she couldn't help but feel a tiny bit of hope.

Chapter Two

The next morning, Cece's journey to China began on a plane from Dallas to Chicago, where it would connect to Shanghai. From there, she would take a flight to Xi'an—her final destination. Her first flight went well. Cece spent some of her time rereading her information packet about the S.A.S.S. anthropology program. A brochure touted the program as one of a kind. Few opportunities allowed high school students to study at the college level in a field like anthropology. In fact, most teens she knew didn't even understand what anthro was, but having Ed Charles—a paleontologist and professor at SMU—as a father had had some influence on her. Whenever he could, he made plans to take her to the most prominent natural history museums in the country. But while her dad loved to talk dinosaurs, Cece found herself more interested in the displays of the various tribes of Native Americans, the models of early hominids, and the artifacts used by ancient civilizations. Sure T. rex was cool in its own way, but it was the notion that the world contained so many cultures that intrigued her most.

A program guide offered more information about Cece's curriculum. Her classes would cover the four major fields within anthropology: language, biological evolution, culture, and archaeology. And all of her classes would focus on China specifically. To Cece, this was an added bonus. She'd be learning something about her own ethnicity— something that was about as foreign to her as Mars.

When Cece wasn't in classes during the week, she'd spend many of the weekends visiting significant points of interest in China, including the Terra Cotta Warriors and Horses, one of the most important archaeological discoveries in the world. Then, during the middle of the program, there was the trip to Beijing, home of the Forbidden City and parts of the Great Wall...and also the home of her orphanage. When Cece finished reviewing her itinerary, she felt full of possibilities. At last, she'd learn more about her home country, even if she didn't find her birth parents. Cece bit her lip. *Even if.*

After the long fourteen-hour flight from Chicago to Shanghai, Cece got off the plane to make her connection to Xi'an. As she walked to the next gate, she took in her surroundings. The Shanghai airport was more modern than Cece had expected. The ceiling rose like a giant metallic sail overhead, and the floors gleamed like no one had ever set foot on them. Yet all around her locals and foreigners rushed past. A lady's voice echoed over the loudspeakers, not a single word intelligible to her until another voice spoke in accented English, translating gates and times of various flights. A burst of excitement rushed through Cece as she walked past dozens of signs written in Chinese script. Restaurants advertised noodles, instead of burgers. Duty-free shops displayed images of Asian faces wearing Revlon and Estée Lauder. Every sight seemed unique and interesting. She wished she could have more time to explore.

She checked in at her gate and boarded her flight to Xi'an, saying good-bye to her brief glimpse of Shanghai. On the plane, Cece found her seat, put her things in the overhead compartment, and settled in by the window for the ninety-minute flight. She yawned; all the travel was catching up with her. She glanced at the empty seat beside her and closed her eyes.

After a while, Cece stirred, nestling her head deeper against something warm and very comfortable. *Wait a second.* Cece sat straight up and stared at a guy sitting next to her who was about her age. "I'm sorry!" She put a hand to her mouth and quickly glanced at his shoulder, hoping she hadn't drooled. *Thank goodness—nothing!*

"That's okay," the guy said. "You can use me as a pillow anytime. I needed an aisle seat, but they stuck me in the middle. Is this all right? I can go back—"

"No, no," Cece said as she studied him longer. His hair was dark and wavy, his skin tan, his eyes exotic. In a word, *hot*. "You can stay. It's fine." Was he Chinese? She wasn't certain.

"Are you sure?"

Cece nodded.

"Thanks." He stuck out his hand. "I'm Will."

"Cece." As they shook, Cece's fingers tingled from his touch.

She quickly let go. "So..." She tried to sound casual as she peeked out the window. "Are we almost there yet?" She could see only clouds.

"Almost," Will said. "It's nearly six Xi'an time."

"Great." Cece turned toward him and smoothed her hair. "Um...so where are you from?"

"A small town in Connecticut called Westland. You?"

"Dallas."

"So do you have relatives in Xi'an?" Will said. "Is that why you're here?"

Cece almost laughed. *Is that a loaded question.* "Yeah, something like that. But I'm here doing an anthropology program."

"Anthropology? Me, too."

"S.A.S.S.?"

"Yeah." Will grinned. His smile was cute. Kind of crooked, with just one dimple in his right cheek. "But I have to admit, it wasn't my idea to apply," he said. "I sorta needed a place to go this summer, and my friend Alex convinced me to do it. By some miracle, I got accepted."

"So you're not into anthropology?" Cece asked.

"I'm not sure. I mean, it sounds cool. Researching fossils and stuff."

"Artif—" Cece started, then stopped. *Don't sound like a know-it-all.* "Yeah, fossils. Cool stuff."

Just then, the captain made an announcement in Chinese over the speakers.

Cece glanced at Will. *Say something else,* she told herself. She looked up. "Do you understand what the captain's saying?"

Will listened for a moment. "I get most of it. We're landing fifteen minutes ahead of schedule. Nothing earth-shattering."

The captain spoke some more, and a flight attendant came on. She made her announcement in Chinese, too, but afterward, translated it into English. "Please turn off all electronic devices. Stow your tray tables..."

"So, your parents didn't teach you the language?" Will said as he raised his seat.

Cece hesitated. She didn't like to advertise she was adopted. "No, not really."

Will rested a hand on his knee. "Yeah, hardly any of my Chinese friends back home speak the language fluently. I guess because a lot of them are second generation."

"Right," Cece said, though she wondered which generation she belonged to. Was she even considered first? Or did she count because her adoptive parents were American? She shifted in her seat. She felt stupid. Shouldn't she know this?

"Is this your first time to China?" Will asked.

Cece shook her head, becoming even more uncomfortable. "No, I was...um...born here."

"Really? So how did you end up in the States? You seem totally Americanized."

Now Cece wished she hadn't said that. She fiddled with the edge of her shirt. "Actually, I'm adopted."

"Oh," Will said.

Thankfully, the captain came on once more, giving Cece an excuse to stare out the window again. She wished she could talk about her past without feeling so weird. Why couldn't she just be *normal* about it?

She heard the landing gear come down.

Will must have sensed her discomfort because he changed the subject. "Well, maybe we'll be in some classes together."

Cece looked over at Will and smiled. "Yeah, maybe."

When the plane finally landed, Will let her into the aisle and helped bring down her carry-on. "Do you know anyone else in the program?" he said. They moved down the aisle.

Cece smiled. "Just you."

"Well, I only came with Alex. I sorta left him in the back when I changed seats. Do you want to meet him?"

"Actually, I...um...have to go to the bathroom." She cringed at her own words.

"No problem," Will said. "Maybe you can meet him later."

Cece nodded. "That sounds great."

Will slowed to a stop in the jetway and let other passengers by. "It was nice meeting you, Cece."

"Same here." Cece smiled, then walked out to the main terminal. *You have to go to the bathroom?! Ugh.* She looked for a sign for the ladies. A lot of them were written in Chinese, but it didn't take long to spot the letters *WC.* She headed in the right direction and pushed open the door. Passing a couple of women waiting for a stall, Cece stood by a mirror and pretended to check her makeup. She tried to shake off her embarrassment. *Why couldn't she mention her adoption without getting upset?* Cece turned on the faucet and ran her hands through the water. Maybe there was so much she didn't know that talking about it reminded her of that. She yanked a paper towel from the dispenser. *But think about why you came here, Cece. You're trying to fix that. Don't be so hard on yourself.* She dried her hands, took a few calming breaths, and tucked her hair behind her ears. She felt better.

After one last look in the mirror, Cece left the restroom, got through customs, and picked up her larger suitcase at baggage claim. Then she walked out the doors into a muggy waiting area where hordes of people waited for passengers. It took only a second to spot the large S.A.S.S. sign held up by a young Asian woman wearing an Adidas shirt. Cece, with her baggage in tow, headed toward the sign. This was easier said than done. Everyone between her and the counselor was in a bigger hurry than she was. Or in no hurry at all. She knew Xi'an had a lot of people, but this was ridiculous! Crossing the fifty feet was like venturing through an obstacle course.

At last, Cece joined the Adidas woman, who checked off her name, then directed her toward a bus parked outside the terminal. Interestingly enough, it was cooler outside than it was inside, but still it didn't feel much different from Texas at the start of summer. No, what was different was the way the air smelled—*really* smoggy. She tried not to inhale too deeply, then boarded the bus. She went straight for the back. She was exhausted, and looking at the other students, she could tell she wasn't the only one feeling that way.

Cece sank into her seat and watched a man in a blazer

come aboard, followed by Will and another guy, maybe his friend Alex, all of whom took seats toward the front. The last to board was the woman who had checked Cece in. The bus pulled out of the terminal, and Cece watched Blazer Guy stand up and grab the bus's microphone. "Hello. I am Mark Crawford, S.A.S.S. anthropology program director, acting-liaison-in-charge for Xi'an University, and counselor for the male half of the group." He gestured at the woman standing beside him. "And this is Shu Wen Shan, or you can call her Jenny. We will work together to make sure you get the most out of your experience here. But first, I'll let Jenny tell you more about herself, and then she'll give you an overview of Xi'an as the bus heads into the city." Mark handed the mike to his colleague.

"Hello, students," Jenny said. "Like Mark said, my name is Jenny Shu. I am a graduate student with Xi'an University, your host school for the program. I am also the counselor for the women's dorm...."

As Jenny spoke, Cece noticed that her English was good for someone who wasn't from the States. She even looked somewhat American in the logo'd shirt and the jeans. But something about the simple way she did her hair or the makeup-less face made her look more Chinese than not. She seemed reserved, practical.

"Right now," Jenny continued, "we are fifty kilometers northwest of central Xi'an...."

Cece turned her attention toward the window. Run-down shacks marked with rusted signs went by. Some had English words on them that made sense, like CHINA TELECOM. And some didn't make any sense at all—HAPPY FISH—for a fish market? Though the buildings weren't architectural prize winners, the road itself was better paved than any at home. Overall, the outskirts of Xi'an seemed to be a mix of old buildings and new superhighways.

None of it seemed familiar to Cece. Of course, she hadn't really expected to remember anything about China, but she had hoped she would connect even just a little with her surroundings. She sighed as she leaned her head against her seat. Maybe in Beijing something would feel right to her.

"Xi'an itself," Jenny went on, "is located in the center of Shaanxi Province. For perspective, I will tell you that Shanghai, China's largest city, is fifteen hundred kilometers due east. And Beijing, China's second-largest city, is twelve hundred kilometers to the northeast. To give you an idea of Xi'an's size, Shanghai has a population of eighteen million. Xi'an has about ten million. So to us, Xi'an is not that big."

Not that big? As far as Cece knew, Dallas had only a million people, and she thought that was huge.

"Xi'an's primary industry is manufacturing," Jenny continued. "But what is most distinctive about the city is its rich history. While Beijing is the political capital of China, Xi'an is the historical capital. It is home to thirteen dynasties...."

It wasn't long before the bus entered the city, and the scenery changed into a sprawling urban metropolis. Though Xi'an wasn't completely modern, there was still an odd contrast between past and present here, too. Brand-new cars and motorcycles shared the streets with bicycles so ancient they'd be antiques in the United States. High-rises made neighbors with older, squatter concrete buildings. Even the people seemed to come from different times: teens with spiked hair shared sidewalks with older people who looked like they just came from a hard day's work in the fields. Most striking of all was a huge stone wall rising above the city, surrounding the center of town like a fort. Cece sat up in her seat to get a better look.

"We are outside Xi'an's city walls," Jenny said. "They were built during the Ming dynasty in the late thirteen hundreds to defend the city, and they are considered to be one of the most complete ancient military systems still standing today. Long ago, the walls encircled all of Xi'an, but as you can see now, the city has expanded and the walls enclose only the center. Take a moment to admire them while we head farther south to the university. This weekend, we will come back and you will learn more about this significant landmark."

Cece gazed at the walls. It was hard not to look at them without thinking about the time it must have taken to make something that big—so ominous and powerful against the city backdrop. She knew instantly the walls would be one of her favorite sights here.

The bus meandered through crowded streets, and a half hour later, it finally came to a stop at Xi'an University. Once Cece got off the bus and walked through a stone gate, she was amazed to see the campus didn't look that different from any community college back in Dallas. It was somewhat spread out, dotted with institutional buildings, a few lawns, and the occasional tree. At this, Cece was somewhat relieved. Given Xi'an's population, she had a feeling space was a commodity here, and XU was probably a lucky school to have something like *grass*.

The men's and women's dorms were in separate buildings. Cece and the rest of the girls followed Jenny while the guys went with Mark. She caught a glimpse of Will as he was walking away, and he happened to look back at the same time. He smiled and waved, and Cece waved back.

In the lobby of the women's dorm, the girls gathered around Jenny for some logistics info: there would be room assignments first, then a welcome dinner at eight thirty, and official orientation tomorrow.

While Cece waited for her assignment, she perched on a bench with her belongings and stole glances at the girls around her. The fact that they were all in an anthropology program didn't really show, though a few of them did look a shade on the geeky side. Some of the students seemed

to know one another, too, but the majority appeared to be as solo as she was, including the tall blonde standing next to her. She wondered why she hadn't put more thought into who her roommate might be, and now she found herself worried about how she looked, how she smelled—she breathed into her hand. Had she brought any gum?

Cece dug in her backpack and her hand closed around a pack of Tic Tacs. *Good enough.* She pulled it out and shook some mints in her hand.

"Mind if I have some?"

Cece looked up. The blonde girl was talking to her.

"Sure." Cece held out the pack.

"Thanks. I owe you one." She gave Cece a wide smile, showing off a perfect set of white teeth. It occurred to Cece that the girl could totally pass for an Abercrombie model with her stunning blue eyes and long legs, shown off in a pair of denim cutoffs. The girl shook a few Tic Tacs into her palm and took a seat next to Cece. "Nothing more disgusting than bus breath, you know?" She popped them into her mouth. "I'm Kallyn. From Colorado."

"I'm Cece. Texas."

"So are you here voluntarily," Kallyn said, "or did someone force you to apply?"

"Voluntarily," Cece said, hoping that was the right answer.

Kallyn looked slightly relieved. "Me, too." She leaned against the wall. "So, what part of anthropology do you like best? Are you more into the physical aspect of it or the cultural?"

"Definitely cultural. What about you?"

"Physical. Last year, I went to a program in northwestern Colorado and got to dig up real arrowheads. The director let me keep one." She pointed to a key chain hanging from her messenger bag. A shiny obsidian arrowhead dangled from the chain.

"How did you manage that?" Cece said.

"My mother is the director." She grinned.

"Miss Charles?" Jenny called.

"That's me." Cece stood, gathered her bags, and turned to Kallyn. "Good luck with your room assignment."

"You, too."

Smiling, Cece went up to Jenny, hoping her roommate would be as cool as Kallyn.

"You will be sharing a room with Jessica Ye," Jenny said, handing Cece a key. "She arrived last night. Very nice girl. Your room is on the third floor. Number 307."

Cece took the elevator up, thinking that "very nice" would certainly do. She stepped out and found the door to her room, smoothed her hair, then went inside. The first thing she noticed was that one of the beds looked slept in. A Gucci purse was resting on top of the sheets.

"Hello?" Cece said.

"Just a second," came a voice from behind a door.

Cece dropped her things onto the empty bed and

unzipped her suitcase. She heard the bathroom door open and turned. An Asian girl with gorgeous, wavy hair stepped out, patting a towel to her face. "Hi, I'm Jessica," she said. "You're...Celise?

"Call me Cece," Cece said.

Jessica put the towel down. "Do you mind that I took the right side of the room. The closet on this side seemed a little bigger, and I have *a lot* of clothes."

"No," Cece said, trying to be polite. "I don't mind." But a part of her sort of did. What if *she* had a lot of clothes?

"So..." Jessica studied her. "Are you Chinese?"

"Uh..." Cece tried not to act taken aback by the question. She wasn't used to people asking her that so directly. She turned to her suitcase and started unpacking. "Yeah, I'm Chinese."

"Great! Me, too. We can totally commiserate together."

"Commiserate?" Cece said, looking back. "Over what?"

"You know, like *everything*?" Jessica sat on her bed and reached for her purse. "Like how our parents are always trying to send us off to math camp or something equally tragic. Can you believe this one though, archaeology?"

"Anthropology," Cece corrected.

"Yeah, whatever." Jessica opened her purse and took out a compact. She started applying powder to her face as she talked. "It's as if they know how *lame* anthropology sounds. You know what my father said to me?" She mimicked his voice. "'Lame is *good*. Lame get you into good school!' Next thing I know, Dad's pulling strings, and I'm on a plane from San Francisco heading to China. Aggravating, isn't it?" She snapped the compact shut.

"I guess," Cece said uncomfortably.

Jessica rummaged through her purse. "So, I noticed that your last name is Charles. Is it your mom or your dad who's Chinese?

Here we go again. Don't act weird. "Actually, I'm adopt-ed," Cece said. "My parents are white."

"Really," Jessica said. She went through her purse again. "Then... if you don't mind my asking, how exactly does that work in your family? Have your parents tried to teach you any Chinese?" She pulled out a tube of lip gloss.

"Not really," Cece replied.

"Well, that's okay. I can totally help." She applied the gloss, and the room filled with scent of strawberry. "What about your friends back home? Are any of them Chinese?"

Cece paused before answering. "No, not many Asians go to my school." In fact, there probably weren't even enough to fill a Volkswagen bug.

Jess looked up. "So what about Chinese culture then? Like how much do you know about customs and stuff?"

Cece stared at Jessica. What was this, *twenty ques-*

tions? "Um...not a whole lot." She immersed herself in unpacking. Once again, the conversation was making her feel inept. And with Jessica, it was even worse than it had been with Will.

"Nothing about culture, huh?" Jessica said. "Well, consider yourself lucky on that front. My parents can't stop reminding me how Chinese I am." She got up and opened the door to her wardrobe. A mirror hung from the inside of the door. She twisted from side to side as she studied her reflection. "Oh, wait, one more thing..." She turned toward Cece. "Would you date an Asian guy?"

Cece nodded. "Yeah, why wouldn't I?"

Jessica's eyes brightened. "Oh, I have so much to teach you. Let's start with rule number one." She started counting off on her fingers. "Never date an Asian boy. Why? First, they're a little too close to their mothers, if you know what I mean. Second, odds are they'll be more interested in computer games than you. And third, nabbing one over five feet eight is like statistically impossible."

Cece frowned. "Aren't you stereotyping though?"

"Call it whatever you want," Jessica said. "I am *so* done with Asian men. Just don't tell my parents I said that."

Someone knocked at the door, and Cece was glad for the interruption.

"That's probably my friend Lisa," Jessica said, getting up. She opened the door and an Asian girl swooped in.

Her hair was cropped short and streaked with blonde. A YSL bag hung from her arm. "Jess, you will *not* believe what my roommate is doing now." She noticed Cece and stopped. "Oh, hi."

"Lisa," Jessica said. "This is Cece."

"Hi." Cece smiled and gave Lisa a little wave.

Lisa smiled back.

"Lisa's parents are friends with my parents," Jessica explained.

"Which means I'm also here against my will," Lisa finished. Then she turned to Jessica and pouted. "Why are *you* always so lucky? While you've got Miss Cuteness, I had to get Sirena." She glanced at Cece. "She just spent ten minutes showing off the *Encyclopaedia Britannica* CD she brought for research." She flopped into Cece's desk chair. "I might have to stay with you guys if the situation gets any worse."

Jessica surveyed the room and shrugged. "Why not? We could get a cot and put it between our desks. If it's all right with you, Cece?"

Both of the girls looked at her.

Cece swallowed. "Um...sure."

"Terrific. Lisa, you now have a backup plan." Jessica checked her watch. "Is everyone ready? They told us to be at the bus at eight fifteen for dinner. We don't want to keep the boys waiting."

Cece grabbed her purse and reluctantly followed the girls. She thought she'd like to have some fun this summer, but going on a manhunt with the Asian Brat Pack wasn't exactly what she'd had in mind.

Well, maybe the food tonight would be good. She loved Chinese.

Cece got on the bus that would take everyone to the restaurant for the program's welcome dinner. As she followed Jess and Lisa down the aisle, she nodded hello to Mark and Jenny in the front and spotted Kallyn a few rows down, talking to a girl who had really short black hair and dark red lipstick. Maybe the girl was her roommate. Before Cece could say hello, Lisa tugged her along. "I think Jess has found us some seats by some very cute guys." She pulled Cece toward the back, where Cece could hear Jessica talking.

"Excuse me," Jessica said, "are these seats taken?"

When Cece saw who Jessica was talking to, her stomach flipped.

Will looked up. "No, go right ahead. Oh, hey, Cece."

Jessica looked at her. "You two know each other?"

"Yeah," Cece said nervously.

Will nodded. "We met earlier on the plane."

"Well, that's nice," Jessica said, sitting down next to Will. "I'm Cece's roommate, Jessica." She gestured toward Lisa. "And that's Lisa."

Will nodded, then glanced at a guy sitting in the row ahead of him. "This is my friend Alex." Alex smiled at the girls, and Lisa promptly plopped into the seat beside him. Will continued with the introductions. "And I've just met Dreyfuss." Across the aisle, a boy wearing a baseball cap nodded toward Cece. "I go by my last name," he said. "Don't ask me about my first. Have a seat."

Cece politely smiled and settled beside him. She made small talk with Dreyfuss, trying to ignore the incessant flirting Jess was doing with Will. Eventually, though, she found it hard to concentrate with Jess's sugary laughter in the background. Cece inwardly groaned. Could her room-mate be any more obvious?

The bus finally came to a halt along a busy road and opened the doors. As everyone exited, Cece found herself on a crowded sidewalk flanked with shops and restaurants. The cacophony of traffic filled her ears, and as she followed her group, she had to be careful not to bump into people trying to get by. Eventually, they stepped inside a restaurant with floor-to-ceiling windows. The fragrance of meats and Asian spices drifted to Cece's nose, making the place seem promising. Several hostesses greeted the group at the doorway. Their uniforms were gorgeous—red satin dresses with mandarin collars and embroidered with a gold bamboo print. They kept saying *"Huanying guanglin,"* which Cece guessed meant "welcome"...or..."go upstairs" since they were all gesturing that way. (She really needed

to learn some Chinese.) Jenny and Mark took the lead and went up a narrow granite stairwell. They followed as the sound of clanking plates and boisterous chatter wafted from the dining rooms. When they finally got to the fourth landing, Cece stepped through the threshold and was taken aback. The room spanned the whole floor. The decor looked distinctly Asian, from the watercolor scrolls hanging on the walls to the rosewood chairs and the red carpeting. Uniformed servers stood by round white-clothed tables.

Under Jenny and Mark's instruction, a line of Chinese people who seemed slightly older than Cece formed along one wall. Cece guessed they were probably their student hosts from XU. Most of them were dressed like any college student in the States—jeans, T-shirts, shorts—and what was interesting to Cece was that most of the girls didn't wear makeup. It was kind of refreshing.

Mark called roll, and one by one, American kids from the S.A.S.S. program, about forty in total, went up to him, pinned name tags to their shirts, and paired up with the local students. After Cece got her name tag, she approached her host, a skinny guy wearing a Houston Rockets shirt. His badge read PETER "SHI YI" LU.

"Hi, Cece, nice to meet you," Peter said in accented English. "You are from Texas, right? Do you like Yao Ming?"

"Um…" Cece said, "Yao who?"

"Basketball," Peter replied. He pointed at his shirt. "The Rockets?"

"Oh." Cece shrugged. "I've never heard of him."

"Never heard of him?" Peter's eyes widened. "You are from Texas and you do not know about the best basketball player in the USA?! You have to learn. I will teach you."

"You will, will you?" Cece said, a smile tugging at her lips. There was something about Peter's goofy nature that was endearing.

"Yes," Peter said, "I will have to tell you all about America." He ushered her toward a table. "I know a lot. Robert De Niro, Tom Cruise, McDonald's..."

Cece laughed as she and Peter sat down. Jessica and Lisa joined her, along with Will, Alex, Dreyfuss, and their hosts. Jessica, Will, and Lisa had been paired with guys. And Alex and Dreyfuss were with girls.

"Thanks for saving us a table," Jessica said as she and her host, George, sat down. George was kind of round and short, and, judging by the way Jessica wasn't even looking at him, she probably wasn't thrilled to be paired with him. Lisa, sitting to George's left, looked far more pleased with her host, Michael—a preppy guy dressed in a polo and khakis.

Soon everyone was seated, and Cece tried to pretend it didn't bother her that Will was now sitting directly across from her, looking especially good in a white button-down. He glanced up at her and smiled. Cece returned the

smile, then quickly turned to talk to Peter again. But at that moment, Mark quieted the room as he stood at the podium. "All right, let's begin, shall we? Welcome to the S.A.S.S. anthropology program. First, I would like to give a big hand to our hosts from our partner program at Xi'an University."

Everyone politely clapped.

"I promise I'll keep this short. The purpose of tonight's dinner is for everyone to get to know one another. Your hosts are college students attending the Intensive English Program, or IEP, at XU. This means your objective will be to help them with their English courses as much as possible. In exchange, they will assist you with your cultural and language studies. You should meet with them as often as you can; they will be as invaluable to you as you will be to them. Now, orientation begins tomorrow. That's Sunday, in case anyone has lost track—ten A.M. There will be an exam tomorrow, so talk with your hosts and start sharing."

"Exam?" Lisa complained. "About what?"

"I have no idea," Dreyfuss said. "But does anyone want to guess what that is?" A server had just placed a platter of what looked like shredded vegetables on the lazy Susan.

"It's carrot and turnip," said Amy, Dreyfuss's host. "Very good. Try." She took some of the veggies, then spun the lazy Susan.

When it came to Cece, she used her chopsticks to ease some onto her plate with grace. If there was one thing she did know about being Chinese, it was using chopsticks. She lifted the veggies to her mouth. Not bad for her first dish in China. It was kind of spicy, a little sweet, a little sour. She went for seconds.

Next, a chef in a white hat pushed a cart to the table. As Cece turned to face the cart, her enthusiasm for authentic cuisine fizzled into the atmosphere. A roasted duck with its head still intact stretched across the cart. The chef picked up the fowl and snapped it at the neck and head. Then he ripped the bill off the duck's face with one quick jerk. Finally, he raised a butcher knife and split the skull into two.

Cece winced.

The chef scooped up the parts, put them on a plate, then set the plate on the lazy Susan.

The duck's broken face was staring right at her.

While everyone watched the chef slice the remaining carcass, Peter said, "Are you okay? It is only Beijing duck. Think Chinese chicken burrito."

Cece nodded weakly.

Peter must have sensed she wasn't okay because he rotated the duck so it was staring at Dreyfuss instead. "Better?"

She nodded again. "Yes, thanks." But her appetite had just left the building.

From that point on, the food situation only got worse. It was as though the menu planner had purposefully picked

the most disgusting things to serve. Cece's idea of a meal did not include a slimy eel coiled on a platter (it looked ready to attack), *live* shrimp drowning in a bowl of wine, or steamed pregnant crabs with orange eggs.

The odd thing was Cece seemed to be the only person at her table affected by the *Ripley's Believe It or Not* meal they were having.

"Don't look sad, Cece." Amy pushed up her glasses with the tip of her finger. "All this, Chinese delicacy. This very special dinner for special occasion. We don't eat every day." She poked at a fish skull with her chopsticks and balanced a glassy eyeball on the tips. She put it to her lips. *Slurp!* "Eyes good for vision."

Will and Dreyfuss grimaced.

Cece's stomach churned.

"Amy, I don't think Cece looks sad," Jessica said. "Try green."

It was too much. Cece got up from the table. She didn't know which way the bathroom was, and her insides were now officially doing the Wave.

"Cece, what's wrong?" someone said.

She covered her mouth. She couldn't stop picturing fish eyes, live shrimp trying to climb their way to safety, broken duck faces.... She saw the blurry image of a door and bolted for it.

Will grabbed her wrist. "Cece, it's that way."

But it was too late.

• • •

In her room, Cece lay in bed on her side, a wadded-up tissue in her hand. Even though she'd brushed her teeth a million times, she thought she could still taste carrots and turnips. She wiped at her mouth.

"It wasn't that bad." Jessica was sitting across from Cece on her bed, gently smoothing moisturizer onto her face. "I mean, Will's khakis weren't all that great. He can pick up another pair here for like five bucks. He said so himself."

Cece moaned. Throwing up all over someone's pants— especially a cute boy's—was not a way to start the program. "I feel like such an idiot."

"Oh, don't worry about it. That room could have used some more excitement. I mean, did you see who my host was—George? The entire time he only said like two words. *Ni* and *hao*."

Cece scrunched her forehead, trying to figure out what the words meant.

Jessica looked at her. "That means, 'How are you?'"

Oh. Cece lay on her back. This and tonight's episode only proved how out of her element she really was.

If Jessica and Lisa hadn't rushed to her side and helped her to the bathroom after she'd hurled, she probably would have crumpled to the floor and cried. But luckily, her new friends proved they weren't just walking, talking Prada hounds. They cleaned her up as best they could, and

Jessica even volunteered to take her back to the dorm in a cab. Cece felt bad for misjudging Jessica earlier.

"I'm really sorry about tonight," Cece said.

"Stop it." Jessica switched off a lamp, and the room got dark. "Let's try to think about today's good parts."

"Good parts?"

"You know, *Will* parts?"

Cece sighed. "What about him?"

"What about him?! The guy is like the next best thing since Russell Wong."

"Who?"

"Russell Wong. *The Joy Luck Club?*"

It didn't compute. "The joy what club?"

"Ohmigod, Cece," Jessica said. "You can't go on like this. *The Joy Luck Club* is only an Asian American movie classic. And Russell's a really famous Chinese American actor. Maybe I need to get you a book or something."

"Wait a second," Cece said. "I thought you didn't like Asian men."

"*Please.* Russell doesn't count. He's tall, he's *fine*, and he can act. Besides, Russell is only half Chinese, like Will, so I can make an exception."

"Will's half Chinese?" Cece said.

"Yeah," Jessica said. "And he told me he can speak Chinese, too. Well, baby Chinese, that is. I'm finding that strangely hot. Anyway, let's get some beauty rest. We want to look good for our men."

"Our men?" Cece said.

"Yeah, Lisa has her host, Michael—he's pretty cute. You can have Dreyfuss, who's not so bad himself. And me, Will. See? It works out perfectly. This is going to be a decent summer yet. 'Night!"

Decent? Cece thought as the room quieted. How could she expect to have a decent summer in China when she could hardly make it through the first day?

She lay in silence, trying to ignore the headache that was coming on. She waited until she could hear the sound of Jessica's deep breaths, then quietly reached inside her purse beside her bed. She took out the picture and let the moonlight from the window illuminate its surface. The image of herself in China had always given her hope that she might reconnect with her past. Now? The idea of visiting an orphanage in a city hours away seemed like mission impossible. Anyone else was more fit to complete her plan—Jessica, Lisa, even half-Chinese Will. But her? Could *she* do it?

Maybe Beijing really was the Forbidden City.

Maybe she should forget about this whole thing.

Cece put away the photo.

Maybe some questions just weren't worth answering.

Chapter Three

Cece dreaded the idea of going to breakfast the next morning, but Jessica insisted.

"Do I really have to go down there?" Cece asked as she finished getting ready. "What if they're serving live crocodiles or something?"

Jessica laughed. "Don't be ridiculous. If I know my Chinese food, it'll be rice porridge or *saobing youtiao*."

"*Youtiao?* What's that?"

"Fried bread dipped in soybean milk."

"Sounds great," Cece said dryly.

"Oh, come on," Jess replied. "It's not that bad. Get in touch with your heritage!"

Cece was about to respond, but was interrupted by a knock at the door.

"Good morning," Peter said to Jessica as she opened the door. He was wearing a shirt that read BORN IN THE USA.

Cece smiled.

"I came to get Cece. Is that all right?"

"Me?" Cece went to the door. "What for?"

"It's a surprise," Peter replied, a gleam in his eye.

Cece looked at Jessica, who shrugged. "He's your host."

"Come on," Peter said. "I did not spend fifteen minutes begging the front-door person for your room number for nothing. You must say yes."

Cece smiled again. "All right." She joined Peter in the hall. Perhaps whatever he had planned would be a step above soybeans in the dining hall. She turned to Jessica. "I'll see you at orientation?"

"Sure," Jessica said. "Lisa and I will save you a seat."

Peter and Cece headed out, leaving the university through the main gate. The city streets bustled with morning activity. Stores were already open, and tons of people were out shopping. Cece walked past a stationery store, a shoe place, and a boutique completely devoted

to women's hair accessories. Street vendors stood along the sidewalk, selling steamed buns and roasted eggs. The energy of Xi'an was invigorating. "Where are we going?" Cece said.

"You will see," Peter said mysteriously. "Just follow me."

Before long, they came to a corner and stood in front of the golden arches—McDonald's! Cece had never seen anything more beautiful in her entire life. Forget Chinese food—she would get in touch with her heritage at lunch.

"Egg McMuffin, anyone?" Peter pushed open the door.

"Excellent." Cece promptly went inside and stood in line. The place was packed with locals. "Man, Chinese people must like this place."

Peter grinned. "A lot of young people here like things from the West. It is a dawn of a new era!" he announced. "I said that right, didn't I?"

Cece nodded as she studied the menu. A breakfast sandwich was almost the same price as in the States. "But isn't McDonald's kinda expensive here?"

"It is. However, Chinese citizens are getting richer. We do not all work in the factories and the fields, you know." He smiled.

"I see."

"But do not be mistaken," Peter went on. "We like our Chinese food, too. I know I will find something local you will like here. However, this morning, I think you need a break, yes?"

Cece let out a breath. "Definitely." It was their turn to place their order, and as Peter spoke with the boy behind the register, Cece was glad she had Peter for a host. Mark had been right. Peter would be invaluable to her experience here. He made everything feel that much more doable.

After a satisfying breakfast, Cece and Peter walked back to the university.

"So why do you like America so much?" Cece said, pointing to Peter's T-shirt. "I mean, I know you explained the Chinese are interested in the West, but I get the feeling you're more enthusiastic than most."

"This is a good question," Peter said. "I have always been a big fan of the USA. My cousin, he lives in Los Angeles. He tells me all about Hollywood. Making movies. One day I will save enough money and go there. I want to apply for film school and direct big blockbuster hits."

"Yeah?" Cece said.

"Maybe you can help me."

"Me? How?"

"You can help me with my application."

Cece shook her head. "Oh, Peter, I know nothing about filmmaking."

"That is not what I mean," Peter said. "You know a lot about English. I want my essays to be perfect." He checked his watch as they approached the gates. "But we can talk about this some other time. You are late."

Cece stopped at the gate. "Thanks for breakfast."

"You're welcome," Peter said. "So maybe I will see you this afternoon? I can show you around. We can see Pizza Hut, KFC, Starbucks...."

Cece laughed. "How about something I can see only in Xi'an."

"Oh, right," Peter said. "I guess we can try that. Let us meet here after orientation. Twelve o'clock?"

"Okay," Cece said.

Peter turned to walk away and waved. *"Zai jian!"*

"Zai jian!" Cece repeated, certain that meant good-bye.

When Cece stepped into the lecture hall, the other program students were already seated. Mark and Jenny were standing in the front along with several members of XU faculty. They welcomed the group. Cece spotted Jessica and Lisa toward the middle, but instead of an empty spot waiting for her, Will and some other guys occupied the seats around them. It was just as well. She'd rather not face Will today after what happened last night. She plopped down by the door and noticed Kallyn was only a couple of seats away.

"Hey," Cece whispered.

Kallyn smiled. "Hey." She was holding a yellow sheet of paper. "They passed this out. You want to share?"

"Sure." Cece moved over, then listened to what Jenny was saying.

"Over the next nine weeks, you will spend six hours in class every day in language, culture, evolution, and archaeology, respectively. The rest of your time can be spent as you wish, unless there is a required excursion or event. We will discuss that when we finish explaining your grades."

"You will notice from your handout," Mark continued, "each of your four classes makes up twenty percent of your grade. The remaining twenty percent comes from a team project."

Cece glanced at the paper Kallyn was holding. It detailed everything hour by hour, the locations of the rooms, the teachers, and a summary of how their grades would be calculated.

"The program is entirely pass/fail," Mark said. "Your grades across subjects are tabulated together. If your average falls below seventy, you do not pass, and you do not receive college credit. Seventy or above, and you're a go. Astound us with something much better than that, and we send you home with a certificate commending your achievements for your parents, *and* we'll give you recommendations to the university of your choice."

Cece listened closely. Any opportunity to get a leg up for college was one she was going after.

"You may be wondering what your team projects are all

about," Mark went on. "Let us show you an example from last year's group."

The lights dimmed as a screen came down from overhead. Opening credits appeared, titling the film: *The Great Wall: Years in the Making.* An American teenager dressed in a spectacularly ill-fitting royal costume spoke Chinese to a crowd of students. Subtitles ran across the bottom of the screen as the film explained how the walls were constructed and how techniques differed from dynasty to dynasty. The students acted it out by first hauling dirt across the set, then bricklike stones, and eventually giant, fat boulders. They also portrayed different leaders of the times, instructing workers to tear down or rebuild the walls to suit their needs. The acting was over the top, but the movie was extremely informative at the same time.

At the film's conclusion, the audience clapped.

"That was pretty corny," Kallyn whispered.

"No kidding," Cece replied. "But the students really seemed to have a handle on their Chinese. It must have taken them weeks to get that down."

"Well, maybe I can be the cameraman," Kallyn said.

"That's exactly what I was thinking," Cece replied.

"As you can see," Jenny said when the lights came on, "you will be making a documentary. This film should address subject matter from at least two of your courses while focused on one specific topic. And you are also encouraged to make it fun."

"That's right," Mark said. "Anthropology doesn't have to be dry and boring. Now, if you turn over your handout, you'll see a calendar of our excursions."

Kallyn flipped the paper over.

"To give everyone time to get comfortable with classes, we'll take our first outing at the end of the program's second week. We'll begin with the major destinations within the city, such as the Bell Tower, the Drum Tower, and the City Walls. Then the following week, we'll see the Terra Cotta Warriors and Horses, located just outside of Xi'an. Right before midterms, we'll take our big trip to Beijing for the must-see Great Wall and Forbidden City, and when we get back, things will calm down, with a few smaller trips to local museums. This way, you have time to prepare for final exams in your classes and complete your team projects.

"Now, one last thing about your free time here. We expect you to spend it as any college student would—however you like—but that means you will also need to be extremely self-directed to stay on task. We're cramming an entire semester's worth of classes into nine weeks, so things move fast here. It's easy to get overwhelmed."

Next Jenny introduced the faculty, four professors who took turns at the podium and discussed their classes and their expectations of the students. Two of them were adjunct professors from the United States who were on an "exchange" of their own with Xi'an University. The other two were local to XU. All of them seemed like standard

faculty material, except for the culture teacher, Professor Hu, who spoke English so poorly, Cece could barely understand her. The fact that the woman was probably seventy-five years old didn't help, either. After Professor Hu stepped down, Kallyn and Cece looked at each other. "Did you get a word of what she said?" Kallyn asked.

"Uh...she kinda lost me at *Hey-ro*."

Kallyn and Cece started giggling, but that quickly ended when Mark said, "Now, Jenny and I are passing out proficiency exams. This was the test I mentioned at dinner last night. I need everyone to sit at least two seats apart." Students started moving, and Cece grudgingly picked up her things and moved to her original seat.

"You have exactly two hours to complete it," Jenny said. "Your performance will determine how we sort you into class sections and assign your project teams."

Cece broke out into a cold sweat as she took the test. It covered everything from the species of the first man discovered in China to "How do you say 'Where is the restroom?' in Mandarin Chinese?" After she turned it in, she was certain she had flunked at least a quarter of it.

"I could eat like a gallon of Rocky Road right now," Kallyn said as they filed out of the lecture hall and into the lobby. "There is no way I passed."

"I'll bring the hot fudge," Cece added.

More students came out of the lecture hall.

"So, where are you headed next?" Kallyn asked.

"I'm supposed to meet my host, Peter, at the gate," Cece said. "He wants to take me around town."

"Hey, me, too. You want to go together?"

"Sure."

"Cece, there you are!" Jessica stepped into the lobby with Lisa. She gave Kallyn a quick look. "Oh, hi!"

"This is Kallyn," Cece said. "Kallyn, meet Jessica, my roommate. And that's Lisa."

"Hello," Kallyn said with a nod.

"Nice to meet you," Jessica said. Then she quickly turned to Cece. "Lisa and I were going to get a massage."

"A massage?"

"Yeah," Lisa said, "it's like eight dollars for two and a half hours of *heaven*. I booked a room for three of us already. But I can add Kallyn if she wants to come."

"Well..." Cece began. She'd never had a massage before, and the idea of lying on a table with some random stranger touching her everywhere totally creeped her out. "Actually, Kallyn and I are meeting our hosts. Do you guys mind if we pass?"

Jessica shrugged. "No, I guess we could change it to two. But you have to be back at the room by eight. We've made *special* plans."

Special plans? Cece could only imagine it had something to do with the guys again. She still wasn't exactly

psyched to see Will, but she couldn't avoid him forever. "Sure, I'll see you at eight."

"Great," Jessica said. "Later, girls!" She and Lisa headed off.

"So Jessica's your roommate," Kallyn remarked. "She seems nice."

"She is," Cece said. "What about your roommate?

"Um... let's just say that the word *weird* doesn't cut it. I knew Angelica and I wouldn't exactly be the best of friends when she started hanging up posters of famous vampires in historical literature all over her side of the room."

"Oh, I see." Maybe she was lucky to have Jessica for a roommate.

They continued walking and met up with Peter and Kallyn's host, James. Everyone made introductions, and it turned out Peter and James already knew each other from a couple of classes together at XU.

"Kallyn and I were thinking all of us could go together today," Cece said.

"Sure," Peter said. "What do you think, James?"

He nodded. "That is a good idea. Maybe we can travel to the city center for lunch?"

Cece liked the idea. She remembered how they'd passed the center of town yesterday on their way from the airport, and she'd love to see what was within the walls. Once everyone agreed, they walked to a nearby stop and got onto a public bus. It was jammed with people, but

Cece somehow managed to stand close enough to a window. She watched as they passed through a large tunnel in a section of the wall. When the bus emerged on the other side, a giant imperial-style building, elevated on a wide stone pedestal, stood at the middle of a roundabout. Cece instantly recognized the structure from her program brochure—the Bell Tower, the symbol of the city. She couldn't wait to visit it when the program took its tour.

The bus stopped, and Peter and James ushered Cece and Kallyn off. As they walked along a crowded street lined with trendy clothing stores and fast-food restaurants, Peter explained they were headed for the Chinese Muslim Quarter, one of the main attractions within the City Walls.

"Chinese Muslims?" Cece said.

"China has a long history of Islam," Peter said. "The quarter is one of the most historical places in Xi'an. You did not know?"

Cece and Kallyn shook their heads.

"Xi'an was the beginning of the Silk Road," James explained. "Many Middle Eastern merchants settled here and they built"—he stared at Peter—"*Qingzhen si?*"

"Mosques," Peter translated.

James nodded. "Yes, mosques. The Muslim Quarter has the largest and oldest mosque in China. It was constructed in the fourteenth century. We will see it after lunch."

Cece nodded. She'd love to see what a mosque that old looked like.

Soon they approached a narrower street marked by a gate with a banner above written in Chinese and English. Cece read, WELCOME TO BEIYUANMEN ISLAMIC STREET. The Muslim Quarter was a feast of sights and sounds. The main thoroughfare was paved with wide rectangular stones that gave the street an old feel, and it was closed to traffic, allowing visitors to stroll the shops and restaurants on either side. Snack carts dotted the walkways, and vendors called for passersby to taste their offerings. Overhead, Cece noticed a number of wooden birdcages hanging from the trees, each inhabitant singing its song. She took it all in, smiling. It was such an interesting place.

"The Muslim Quarter has some of Xi'an's best and most authentic cuisine," James boasted as they approached a restaurant.

Hearing the word "authentic" made Cece feel uncertain, but as they stepped inside, Peter whispered, "Don't worry. You will like this food—no heads, no eyes." Cece smiled weakly and entered the restaurant. The place smelled inviting, like a home-cooked meal of pot roast baking in the oven. They took a seat at a long cafeteria-style table, and Peter and James ordered for Cece and Kallyn. Within minutes, giant bowls of a broth soup lay before them. "We are having *yangrou paomo*," Peter said. "It is a traditional Xi'an Muslim dish." The server set down a plate of white bread that looked like pitas.

"The bread is called *mo*," James said.

"You break it into your soup, like this." Peter ripped the bread into bits and dropped them into his bowl.

Cece and Kallyn did the same. Cece watched as the pieces expanded, soaking up the flavors of the soup.

"Now eat," Peter said.

Following his lead, Cece picked up her chopsticks and loaded her plastic spoon—a little bread, some vegetables, a piece of lamb. Then she scooped it into her mouth. Her tongue tasted an amazing combination of flavors she'd never encountered before. The broth was tangy, spicy, rich.... Maybe she *would* like some of the food here after all.

Afterward, Cece paid for her share, which came to about twelve yuan, less than a $1.50 in the United States. As they all stepped outside, James said, "Now we will take you to see some history."

They didn't have to walk far before they arrived at the Great Mosque. The architectural elements of the mosque were nothing like Cece had expected. She remembered what a mosque was supposed to look like from a global history class she had taken in school, and this wasn't it. Instead of domes and minarets, this mosque looked very Chinese, with many of the buildings built like pagodas.

In the courtyards, tourists and locals milled about. A prayer hall toward the rear of the mosque was large enough to hold hundreds of worshippers. As Cece took a picture of the courtyard with the hall in the background,

something in the corner of the frame caught her eye. She spotted a young Asian girl who reminded her of herself when she was a toddler. The girl had the same blunt haircut and was holding a Popsicle. Her mother was resting on a bench, plastic bags of groceries beside her, enjoying the solitude of the area. The girl hopped from one stone tile to the next, like she was playing a game of hopscotch. Cece lowered her camera and suddenly wondered what it would have been like if she had grown up here. With her birth mother looking on. Smiling at her like that.

"Hey, Cece," Kallyn said, interrupting her thoughts. "Are you ready to move on?"

Cece turned toward Kallyn, who was now standing beside her. Peter and James were by one of the gates as if they were ready to leave.

"Yeah," Cece said, giving the little girl one last glance. She quickly took a picture of the hall and followed Kallyn toward their hosts.

"Who is up for some bargain shopping?" Peter said as they left the mosque.

"I'm in," Cece said.

Kallyn rubbed her hands together. "Me, too."

"Great, then we are in the right place," James said. "The Muslim District holds the largest souvenir market in Xi'an."

Peter and James led them to a network of alleys just behind the restaurants they had passed earlier. Cece couldn't believe what she saw. One minute, they were standing in a peaceful mosque, and the next, every square inch of her visual field was filled with dozens of stalls carrying merchandise—knockoff Gucci and Prada hand-bags, Polo shirts, jackets, suitcases. In addition to the fakes, every tchotchke imaginable was available, including chops—jade stampers that were used to seal documents with red wax—ivory Buddhas, miniature mahjong sets, and statuettes of the Terra Cotta Warriors.

"Hey, Cece..." Kallyn stopped by one of the stalls. She held up a very good copy of a North Face windbreaker. "This would be perfect for my boyfriend—Ryan's so out-doorsy. But do you think if I gave this to him, it would be too much? Like too *personal*?"

"How long have you been going out?"

"Only a few months," Kallyn said.

"Maybe you should get something like this instead?" Cece held up an empty wooden box with a dragon carved into the top. "I think this says, dating *with possibilities*."

The sales guy nodded in agreement, even though he probably didn't understand a word Cece had said.

Kallyn smiled. "I think you're right."

After Kallyn paid for the box, they shopped some more, and Cece let Peter bargain down a set of silk place mats for her mother, an antique-looking lock for her father, and a silk-embroidered handbag for Alison.

On the way back to the university, the four of them

packed onto a bus, and once again, it was so crowded they had to stand.

"Did you have a good day?" Peter asked.

Cece nodded as she and Kallyn tried to stay on their feet. The bus came to a sudden halt, probably to avoid another bicyclist. "I've loved everything but the transportation," Cece said, trying to dislodge Kallyn's elbow from her ribs.

Kallyn sighed. "I second that."

The group grew quiet for a moment, and Cece thought more about the day. She remembered the young girl she had seen at the mosque, and renewed hope welled up within her. Perhaps she *would* learn something about herself while she was in China. She glanced at Peter and smiled. It had been a good day. A great day, and she still had a whole evening to go.

After a short nap, Cece was ready to go out again and experience more of the city. That night, Jess's special plans turned out to be going to a club with Will, Lisa, Michael, and Dreyfuss. They hailed two cabs to their destination, and along the way, Cece felt optimistic about the evening. She'd decided she'd listen to Al's advice and have a little fun. When they got to the club, the energy inside the place was infectious. Techno music thrummed in Cece's ears as laser lights swept the two-story building. The closest thing to a club she had been to was a teen place in Dallas, and it was so lame, Al and Cece had sworn they'd never go again. But this place was amazing. The people were more sophisticated, and the music was infinitely better.

Though Cece wasn't as skilled in the art of gyrating as Jess and Lisa, she definitely held her own on the dance floor. She even caught Will's eye and smiled, hoping that maybe he had managed to put the previous night's vomiting episode out of his mind. Will smiled back, and Cece felt forgiven. She started to maneuver herself closer, eager to talk to him and maybe get to know him better, but suddenly, Jess was shimmying in front of him, whispering in his ear. Cece felt a twinge of jealousy, but she kept smiling and acted like it didn't matter. Then she saw Lisa snuggling up to Michael, leaving Cece and Dreyfuss dancing with each other. And Dreyfuss looked just a little too excited by the opportunity. Cece knew she had to do something to ensure they stayed just friends.

"Hey Dreyfuss, I think I'm going to sit this one out." Dreyfuss nodded, looking crestfallen.

"I guess that's my cue to get something to drink." He smiled wanly, then headed to one of the bars.

Cece sat at a nearby table, and soon after the song finished, she saw everyone—except for Will—head for one of the bars. Will glanced in Cece's direction, then started walking over.

Cece straightened.

"Hey, Cece," Will said. "Is everything okay?"

Cece tried to look casual. "Yeah. Just needed a break."

"I could use a break myself," Will said. "Do you mind if I sit?" He grabbed the seat beside her, then paused. "Wait a second, you're not going to throw up on me again, are you?"

Cece laughed. "No, you're safe. I'm so sorry about that."

Will sat down, then rubbed his palms against his jeans. "So I know this is going to sound weird," he began, "but there's something I wanted to say to you...."

Cece's pulse quickened. "Really? What's that?"

"I'm sorry I made you feel uncomfortable. On the plane? About you, uh, being adopted?"

"Oh." Cece fidgeted in her seat.

"I just assumed—"

"No," Cece said. "There's no need to apologize. I'm the one who got all weird. I guess I'm a little...I don't know—"

"You don't have to explain," Will cut in. "Why don't we start over instead?" He held out his hand. "Hi, I'm Will."

Cece took in a cleansing breath, then smiled as they shook. She tried to ignore the tingles that marched up her arm. "Nice to meet you, Will. I'm Cece."

"So...what do you hope to get out of the program, Cece?"

Cece laughed again. "Now *this* is a real conversation."

"Hey, it's safe, isn't it?" Will said. "Now spill it."

Cece looked at him. "You really want to know?"

"Actually, I do."

"*Okay.* I guess it'd be nice to learn more about the country I was born in. It'll be good for me. Plus, I think I might be a curator for a museum one day, and the program seemed like a perfect fit." She tilted her head at Will. "And what about you? I mean, I know an anthropology program wasn't exactly your idea, but do you have any hopes for the summer?"

Will smiled. "I have a few...."

"Such as?"

"I can't divulge them all." He looked at her, then glanced away. "At least not yet."

Whoa. Did one of those hopes have something to do with her? She couldn't be sure.

"Well, perhaps you can tell me at least one of them."

"Now we're getting personal," Will quipped as he leaned toward her. Their knees accidentally touched for a moment, and a jolt of electricity shot through her.

"I'm listening," Cece said.

"All right. I'll play. Remember how I said I needed to get away this summer?"

Cece nodded.

"Well, the truth is, my dad is splitting up with my mom, and he doesn't want me around when he breaks the news."

"Oh, no. I wasn't expecting that." She got serious for a

moment. "So then you're hoping they stay together?"

Will chuckled. "Uh, not exactly. I'm a realist, not delusional. I just hope things turn out okay in the end, you know?"

"I see," Cece said. "Will, I'm sorry."

"Now *you* don't have to apologize. Besides, I'm glad to be here. China will be good for me, too."

They sat there for a moment, and neither of them said anything. Then Cece glanced at Will, and she realized her nervousness had all but disappeared. She was comfortable around him.

"Since we're getting...um...personal," Cece said, "you want to know the other reason I'm here?"

"There's more?"

"Mmm-hmm."

"Shoot."

"Well..." Cece tucked a loose strand of hair behind her ear. "One of the reasons I came here was to look for my birth parents."

"Wow," Will said. "That's big."

"Yup."

"This is sort of interesting, isn't it? My family is splitting up, and you're trying to reunite with yours."

"Yeah," Cece said.

"So...do you have any idea where you'll start looking?" Will asked.

"Actually—"

"Will, Will!" Jessica said, interrupting the conversation. "Where have you been?" Her eyes were excited, and her hair looked a little tossed. A drink sloshed in her hand.

"You've got to dance another song with us out there. Lisa found a great spot next to the speakers." She tugged on Will's arm.

Will gave Cece a quick look, then turned to Jess. "Are you okay?"

"Totally. Come on! Let's go."

"All right," Will said, laughing. "I'll talk to you later, Cece?"

Cece smiled and nodded as Jess pulled Will onto the floor. As he walked onto the dance floor, she tried to make sense of her conversation with him. He'd seemed honest, for sure. Open and interested. And now, as she watched Jess throw herself at him, she guessed that he was probably dancing with her roommate only out of politeness.

But still, she wished *she* was the one out there dancing beside him.

Chapter Four

Cece woke up the next morning and immediately groaned. She had slept through her alarm and woke up a half an hour late. She glanced at Jess's bed, which was empty. *Hmm,* even Miss Forced-to-Be-Here was up earlier than she was.

Cece hurried to get ready to make it to class on time, and when she left her room, she noticed Jessica on the phone in the hall. She was speaking Chinese. Cece paused and signaled to Jess, wondering if she should wait so they could head out together. Jess covered the phone with her hand and whispered. "Go on without me. It's my dad. Classes haven't even started, and he's already on my case." She rolled her eyes, then went back to speaking on the phone.

Cece nodded and made her way to the academic building to her Chinese I language class. When she stepped inside, she realized she was actually early. The teacher hadn't arrived yet, and only a handful of students were there. She spotted Kallyn and sat in the seat behind her.

"Hey, Kallyn," Cece said.

"Hey. You look pretty wiped. What did you do last night?"

Cece took out her notebook from her backpack. "We just went clubbing."

"Oh?" Kallyn said. "With Jess and Lisa?"

"Yeah, and a few guys."

Kallyn smiled. "Sounds exciting."

Cece thought about her conversation with Will. "It was fun. What did you do?"

"Enh…" Kallyn played with the pen in her hand. "I just grabbed dinner in the dining hall and met a few people from the program. Nothing mind-blowing."

More students filtered in.

"Maybe next time you'll come with me," Cece said.

"Clubbing? Nah, that sorta thing is lost on me. Now that I'm with Ryan it seems kinda pointless, you know?"

"Then something else."

"Sure."

At that moment, the language professor strolled in with a mug of coffee in his hand and an arm loaded with files. He set down his things on a nearby desk and surveyed the room. "...*jiu, shi, shi yi, shi er.* Twelve. Good. Everyone is here. Let me start off by saying, *Zao.*"

The professor waited as though the class was supposed to respond. No one said a word.

"Okay, I see we've got lots of work to do. I am Professor Sutton, your Chinese I instructor. You all have been assigned to this section because, as you might have guessed, you failed the language portion of the proficiency exam."

A couple of sighs could be heard throughout the room.

"Oh no," Professor Sutton said, "don't be disappointed. This is good. You are clean slates. Unlike some of your Americanized counterparts in the other sections, you actually have a shot of having a perfect accent."

At this, Cece brightened. Maybe there was an upside to being as clueless as she was. She reveled at the idea of speaking Chinese flawlessly.

"But let me be clear," Professor Sutton continued. "Over the course of this summer, you will not only learn how to order food or hail a cab, you will also learn about the origin of the Chinese language and how the language distinguishes itself from others around the world. By taking this class, you will get a basic understanding of how to describe written and spoken communication in the context of the study of humanity—that is anthropology. Does everyone understand?"

"So basically," a girl said, "we're going to learn why Chinese uses characters and why other languages use letters?"

"Something like that," Professor Sutton said.

A couple of the students nodded. Someone yawned.

"All right, let's start off with *phonology....*"

When class was over, Cece's head was swimming. She had just been told that in a few days, she needed to learn pinyin, a Romanized system designed to help students learn Chinese pronunciation using alphabetic letters. Then to learn how to read and write, Cece would have to practice writing the individual strokes that made up each *zi*, or character, until it was committed to memory. Finally, each day they'd be assigned a new vocabulary list. She would have to stay on top of it all, or there would be no way she'd pass.

Cece attended her next two classes, evolution and archaeology, where she felt much more comfortable. In fact, she was familiar with most of the basic material, but she'd still have to put in some effort to do well—there'd be papers to write and plenty more to memorize. But when she got to her culture class, she immediately knew it would be a much tougher challenge. Without even a greeting, Professor Hu paced the aisle and suddenly stopped in

front of Cece's desk. "Tell me. Where fortune cookie come from?" she asked, peering at Cece through her Coke-bottle glasses.

Cece was completely caught off guard. "Um..."

"Wrong," Professor Hu said. "America. How many of you know this already?"

No one raised his hand.

Professor Hu smiled, but her grin looked kind of evil. "And this is why you are in my class."

She got right down to business, returning to the chalk-board and writing two words: *Final paper.*

Cece turned to Kallyn and mouthed, *She's talking about finals already?*

Kallyn shrugged, looking just as horrified as Cece.

"I expect big paper at end of term. You pick something in Chinese culture that influence human behavior today. Example be religion, pop culture, holiday, what you please. But you must apply theory from class to your paper. Worth forty percent of grade. I give you time to think about what you write." She wagged her finger at everyone. "Topics due in six weeks." She tossed her piece of chalk into the tray.

Cece swallowed. Forty percent on *one* paper?

When the day ended, Cece and Kallyn walked out of the academic building together. "Can you believe all this intense work?" Kallyn asked.

"I know. I love evolution and archaeology, but language and culture are going to be tough."

"Man, I wish Ryan were here," Kallyn said.

"Yeah?" Cece said as they crossed the lawn.

"He'd love this program. He's as into anthro as I am." Kallyn stopped to lift the flap of her bag. An oval pin of Kallyn and her boyfriend was stuck to a pocket underneath. "Cute, isn't he?"

Cece nodded.

"What about you, Cece? Do you have a boyfriend back home?"

"Not exactly. The guys who like me are always...well... a little weird."

"*Hmm.* Well, there are plenty of guys to choose from here. What about Will?"

Cece turned. "What about Will?" she said, a little nervousness creeping into her voice.

"Hey, Cece!"

Cece turned to see Will trotting up to her, a couple of textbooks under his arm.

"Hmm, what about him?" Kallyn whispered, a grin on her face. Then she spoke louder. "Well, I'm off to meet... uh...James for lunch. Bye!" She left so quickly Cece hardly had a chance to say good-bye.

Will caught up with her. "Hey, I was bummed that you aren't in any of my classes."

"Really?" Cece said.

"Yeah.... Look, I wanted to talk to you." He ran his fingers through his hair, and Cece stared at those dark gorgeous

waves. So cute. "I was kind of hoping you wouldn't share with anyone what I said last night. About my parents?"

"Oh, of course," Cece said. "And um...maybe it's a good idea to keep my plans for Beijing quiet, too."

"Sure. No problem, but I was wondering..." He shifted his books from one arm to another. "Aren't you going to need some help? I was thinking about it last night..."

He was thinking about me last night?

"And if you need anything, just ask. Okay?"

Cece's heart pounded in her chest. "Same here," she said. "I mean if *you* ever need to talk or whatever..."

"Right, thanks." Will smiled. "Well, I have to meet up with the guys. So I'll see you later?"

"Um, yeah."

"Great." He took a few steps backward and waved with his free hand, then turned and headed off in the opposite direction.

When Cece returned to her room, she finally got around to checking her e-mail. She'd been gone for only two days, but she knew there would be at least a couple of messages from her mother wondering why Cece hadn't contacted her. She opened her laptop and logged in. Yup, two e-mails from Mom—both titled: *Where are you?*, and one from her dad, saying *WRITE YOUR MOTHER.* Cece typed up a short message, letting her mom know everything was fine.

Then she opened an e-mail from Alison.

To: cece2me@e-mail.com
From: alisofine@e-mail.com
Subject: So?????

Hey Cece,

So???? What's it like there? Is it everything you'd hoped it would be?

Who's your roommate? I bet you're already making loads of friends and you've forgotten all about me because WHY ELSE HAS IT TAKEN YOU SO LONG TO E-MAIL? Helloo?!

By the way, the summer season at Six Flags started off with a terrific bang. Get this: Eugene got fired! Security caught him with $3000 tucked away in his socks and UNDERWEAR. GROSS.

Hurry up and write back!

Al

Cece couldn't believe it. *Now* Eugene gets fired?

She wrote to Alison and gave her an update of her stay in China so far, including the vomiting episode, her trip to the Muslim Quarter, the club, and finally all the details about Will she could give. Writing about him—the way he looked, talked, what he'd said—made Cece wonder if she'd met the perfect guy at last. When she finished her e-mail, she closed the laptop and sighed with satisfaction.

Chapter Five

For the next couple of weeks, Cece had to follow a tight routine to keep up with her classes and intense workload. Mark hadn't been kidding about cramming an entire semester into one short summer. If she wasn't in class, she was working with Peter over lunch or studying with Kallyn. Cece hardly had time to think about Will, and, more important, she hadn't made any progress with her plans for Beijing.

But finally, on a Friday, just before Cece had to go to the lecture hall to get her team project assignment, she stole a few moments to try to locate the orphanage in Beijing.

She sat at her desk, blew air at her bangs, and opened her laptop.

Cece went to Google's mapping site and typed in the address she had for the orphanage. She quickly discovered the Web site didn't cover China, but found a link for Google's China mapping site instead. She clicked on the link and a map of China came up, with Chinese labels all over it. Not a word of English. Cece frowned. It could take her months to understand it. She went to a blank field at the top, entered the address, and clicked a button. Hardly anything on the screen changed. The map of China was still there, but this time, several lines of Chinese characters came up on the left. Cece squinted at the screen, recognizing only a few words, but not enough to understand it. She sighed. Maybe she had to enter Chinese characters instead of letters. She stared at the alphabetic keys on her laptop. Good luck with that one.

Cece stared at the screen, wondering what to do next.

She then tried to find a plain old map of Beijing online, one that was in English. But everything she found turned out to be too basic—tourist maps essentially—without nearly enough detail to locate anything but temples, palaces, and gardens.

Cece rubbed her eyes. How could something so simple be this hard? She glanced at the calendar on her desk. She had three weeks to go before Beijing. *Three weeks.*

Could she learn enough of the language to get herself there and then ask questions?

A wave of nervousness swept through her.

Maybe she should ask Peter for help. Surely he could figure this out.

Maybe she could even get him to go with her.

Hopeful, Cece got up. She'd broach the subject with Peter during their study session at lunch. She grabbed her backpack and left for the lecture hall.

When she arrived, she took a seat next to Kallyn.

"So where's Jessica?" Kallyn asked.

Cece looked around. She spotted Will, sitting with some guys on the opposite side of the hall, but no Jess. Or Lisa for that matter.

"Maybe she's at another massage session?" Cece said. "Or shopping?"

"I wonder how she keeps up with everything," Kallyn mused.

"Me, too." Over the past couple of weeks, Jess had gone out a lot. She regularly asked Cece to come with her, but lately, Cece had declined the invitations, worried she wouldn't get things done for her classes. Plus, she wasn't fond of watching Jess be so flirty with Will all night. So when exactly *did* Jess study? "Maybe she's secretly a genius or something."

Kallyn raised an eyebrow. *"Right..."*

"Well, perhaps it's easier for her because she's got the Chinese part down."

Kallyn looked like she was considering this. "True."

Just then, Mark took the podium. "*Zao*, everyone! I hope you've had a great couple of weeks at XU. The professors tell me we've got a bright bunch this year, which means I know team projects will be better than ever. Jenny is handing out the assignments and a description of the requirements. And before anyone asks, there will be no switching. The teams were handpicked according to your proficiency exams, so that some of our weaker students will be paired with the most learned. This ensures a fair playing ground for all. Now I'll give you a few moments to read over your team assignments."

Jenny came to Cece's row and gave her a stack of papers. Cece took one and passed the rest down. She scanned the sheet for her name. There it was, under Team 3; next came Alex's name, then Will's...Cece's heart skipped. Then she saw Jessica's name, and her enthusiasm dissipated. No doubt Jess would be excited by the lineup, too.

"Darn," Kallyn whispered. "You're not on my team."

"I know." Cece found Kallyn's name under Team 6. Kallyn looked over the list some more. "Hey, that guy Will is on your team." She gave Cece a nudge, and Cece smiled nervously.

"So you like him, huh?" Kallyn said.

"I don't know...maybe."

"Go, you," Kallyn said with approval.

At that moment, Mark started talking again, and Cece turned her attention toward the front. "I want you all to split up into your groups. Team One, please take the first row. Team Two, the second, and on down the line. I'll give you a few moments to get situated, say your hellos, and then we'll begin again."

Cece and Kallyn got up and started moving toward their rows.

"Try not to drool," Kallyn whispered.

Cece smiled, rolling her eyes, and headed to the third row. She took a seat next to Will and tried to act like being mere inches from him wasn't going to give her a panic attack. Since the night at the club, they hadn't really talked without Jessica around.

"So is it you?" Will said.

Cece glanced around nervously. "Uh, is what me?"

"You know," Will said, smirking, "our team's weakest link."

"Oh." Cece blushed. "Well, I *did* flunk the language part of the exam."

"Just the language, huh? That's nothing. I screwed up both the evolution and archaeology sections."

"I guess it's you then," Cece said playfully. Before Will

could respond, Alex and a guy Cece hadn't met yet joined the row.

"Hey, Alex," Will said. "What's up, Chris?" The boys sat beside him.

Will looked over at Cece. "You know, I think I know the answer to our question. Chris has to be the deadweight on our team. Am I right?"

"Yup," Chris said. He was a stocky guy with a super-deep voice to match his physique. "I slept through the exam, if you have to know the truth." He pointed at Alex. "From what I understand, this one's the nerd."

Alex tried to look innocent. "Since when is it a crime to have a high GPA?"

"It's not," Chris said. "It's just, you know, *nerdy*." He looked at Cece. "You're Jessica's roommate, right?"

"Yup," she said. "I'm Cece."

"Chris. Nice to meet you."

"Where is Jess anyway?" Will said.

"I'm not sure," Cece said.

Just then, she heard Jess calling her name. "Cece!"

Will and Cece both looked back.

Jessica was hurrying down the aisle, waving a copy of the team list in her hand. "We're on the same team. I can't believe it." She sat next to Cece. "Sorry I'm late, guys. Lisa lost an earring in the middle of the lawn, and it took for-ever to find it. Did I miss anything?"

Will smiled. "Not yet."

Cece looked at Will and Jess, and inwardly sighed.

"All right, everyone," Mark interrupted. He waited for the room to quiet. "On the back of your team list you will see project topics."

Cece flipped her paper over and scanned the list: The Silk Road and Its Influence on Xi'an's Inhabitants Today. Burial Rituals of the Banpo. The Peking Man and the Theory of Evolution...almost any of them would be great to work on, but the one that caught her eye was Qin Shi Huang: The First Emperor of China.

"The main goal this morning," Mark continued, "is for your team to rank your top three choices and turn those in. This should go fairly easily. In the future, however, you should plan on spending every Friday developing your documentaries. Also, Jenny will be handing out camcorders next week, and if you need props, XU's theater department can loan some to you.

"Finally, keep in mind that you will be graded on demonstration of knowledge, creativity, and teamwork. Your projects will be presented and critiqued during the last day of the program. Good luck."

"So, what do you all think?" Alex said.

"I really don't have a preference for a topic," Jessica replied. "Do any of you?"

Chris shrugged. "Not really."

"Burial Rituals sounds interesting to me," Will said.

"The Peking Man would be great," Alex said.

Cece studied the list again. "I was thinking we should go for the Emperor Qin Shi Huang."

"Really?" Will said, looking at her intently. "Why?"

Cece swallowed, surprised that he would be so interested in her answer. "Well, from what I know, the guy practically built China all on his own. Plus, he was responsible for the army of Terra Cotta Warriors. So the topic seems fun to explore...." She inwardly groaned. Did she have to sound so geekish? "I mean, that is, if you're into that sorta stuff."

"Sounds good to me," Will said.

"We would have a lot of material to work with," Alex added.

"All in favor of the Emperor raise your hand," Jessica said.

Everyone raised a hand.

"Terrific. We'll make Burial Rituals number two, and the Peking Man number three." She sat up in her chair. "Now who wants to get some bubble tea?"

"I'm in," Alex said.

Chris looked confused. "What's bubble tea?"

"They're these drinks that come in all flavors," Jessica said, "like mango, red bean, and grass jelly. And you can get them with gooey tapioca balls at the bottom."

He stared at her. "And people drink that?"

Jess laughed. "Yeah. And I saw a cool place the other

day just a couple of streets away. Let's go, guys." She turned to Cece. "You're coming with us, right?"

Cece glanced at Jessica, then Will. Did she really want to spend the morning witnessing Jess hanging all over Will? But she couldn't say no. She didn't want to seem like a drag either. "Uh, sure."

"All right then," Jess said. "Let's go."

As they walked out of the lecture hall, Cece tried to ignore Jess happily chatting away with Will. But Cece couldn't stop herself from feeling annoyed once more. This time, though, she was more irritated with herself than her roommate. Why was it that whenever she and Jess were in the same room, it was Jess who always seemed more intriguing, more vibrant? The night at the club, Cece had told herself that Will was just tolerating Jess's advances out of politeness, but now she wasn't so sure. He seemed genuinely to like her. And why wouldn't he? Jess was so many things Cece wasn't. So girly-girl, so spontaneous, so...confident.

It made her wonder if she could ever be like Jess.

Cece sighed as Jess casually slipped an arm through Will's.

Doubtful.

That afternoon, Cece put aside thoughts of Will and Jess when she arrived at a local noodle shop to meet with Peter. The place was a favorite of XU's students, not only for its inexpensive food but also for its work-friendly atmosphere. After they ate, Peter and Cece spread out their books, and Cece began her character studies for Professor Sutton while Peter prepared for an English quiz.

"I am almost finished with my practice questions," Peter said. "Have a look." He scooted a piece of paper across the table.

Cece studied the paper. Peter had been working on the past perfect tense. She took her pencil and made some corrections. "Peter, I think you need to review your irregular verb list again. The past participle for forgot is forgotten."

He frowned. "I guess I had *forgotten.*"

She smiled. "Now you're getting it." She returned the paper to Peter and went back to writing a Chinese character in her notebook. "Peter," Cece said, "can I ask you something?" She tapped her pencil against the table. "How do you remember all these strokes?"

Peter looked up. "You write, and write, and write...but sometimes you can look at the word and think of something that reminds you of it."

He pointed at one of Cece's vocabulary words. "You see this one? *Zhong?* It means 'center.' So when you think of center, think of a field." He drew a rectangle on his paper. "Then draw a line down the center of the field. And you have *center.* See?"

Cece cocked her head as she stared at the word Peter

had written. "Hmm. I've never thought of it that way."

"A lot of Chinese words are like something you can see or imagine. They are not just pulled out of a cap, you know."

"You mean hat. Pulled out of a *hat.*"

Peter smiled. "Right, hat."

Cece looked at the next word on her list and tried to use Peter's technique. The word was *da*, which meant big. It looked like a star, so she pictured a big burst of light in the sky. Then she wrote it down. *Da.* The final product almost looked like an asterisk. She compared her character to the real character on the list and noticed she had drawn too many lines. She bit her lip, frustrated just as she had been with the Google map earlier in the day. She glanced at Peter, thinking that maybe she should bring up the orphanage. It seemed like as good as time as any.

"Peter?" Cece said. "I was wondering if you could help me with something."

He looked up. "Which character is it?"

"No, it's not that," Cece said. "It's not even related to S.A.S.S. actually."

Peter paused, his face turning serious. "What is it, Xiao Mei?"

Hearing Peter call her that made her smile. Since he was a few years older than Cece, he'd taken to calling her his little sister. That would also make Peter her Da Ge, or big brother.

"Well...I can trust you, right?"

Peter looked surprised. "Of course, you can. I'm Da Ge."

"Then maybe I should start from the top." Cece took a breath. "First, you should know I'm adopted."

"Adopted?" Peter said. "From here?"

Cece nodded.

"And what is troubling you about that?"

She considered Peter's question. How would she even begin? There was so much that bothered her. For starters, it would be nice to know who her birth parents were. What they looked like. What they were like. But mainly, it was the same old question she had posed to her parents years ago. "I think what's bothering me the most is that I want to know why my birth parents gave me up. I feel like I need to know the truth."

"And what do your American parents say?" Peter said. "Do they have an opinion?"

"They seem to think I was abandoned because I'm a girl. They told me about China's one-child policy and how a lot of parents here want boys."

"And you don't believe that."

"Well, I don't know. It sounds so...cold," Cece said. "I mean, you're from here. Do you think that's the reason why?"

"I am not an expert on this subject," Peter said, "but it is a possibility. However, you can never know the truth unless you hear it from the donkey's mouth."

Cece smiled. "You mean horse, straight from the horse's mouth."

"Right, horse." Peter wrinkled his forehead. "English sayings are so confusing."

"Anyway, that's what I was thinking," Cece said. "I need to hear it for myself. And I thought I'd start with the orphanage. Maybe they can tell me something."

"Do you know where it is?" Peter said.

"Well, that's where you come in. I have the address, but I can't figure out where it is, and I think I'm going to need a translator when I get there, too."

"I see." Peter leaned back in his chair. "Let me think for a moment...."

Cece watched him intently.

"Okay," Peter said. "I'm in."

Cece perked up. "Really?"

He nodded. "You think I would let you wander in foreign country with *your Chinese*? I may be crazy, but I am not stupid." He laughed.

"Gee, thanks."

"No problem. What is Da Ge for?"

Cece grinned, then sat back, relieved that was settled. "So you *have* to let me do something in return. You name it."

"Anything?" Peter said.

"Uh-huh."

Peter went through his backpack and pulled out a folder. "I think I have something." He opened the folder and handed Cece a few sheets of typewritten paper. "These are essays for my film school application."

"Oh, yeah," Cece said, remembering what Peter had said about them when they first met. This would be perfect.

"There are three questions," Peter said, "and I am very stuck."

Cece quickly scanned what Peter had written so far. The grammatical errors were everywhere, and many of the words he had chosen to express his thoughts were incorrect. In fact, it read so awkwardly she could hardly understand what Peter was writing about.

"How is it?" Peter said nervously.

"Um...when is this due?"

Peter groaned. "A couple of months. It's like a bad dream, right?"

"You mean nightmare."

Peter threw his hands up. "You see? I give up."

Cece giggled. "Don't worry, Peter. I can totally help."

"Are you sure?"

Cece returned the papers back to the folder. "Hey, what is Xiao Mei for?"

Chapter Six

After Cece finished her session with Peter, she returned to her room, where she found Jessica standing in front of her closet. Clothes were scattered all over her bed—minis, tank tops, glitter this, sparkly that. "Hey, Cece, are you coming with us tonight? Lisa, Will, Dreyfuss, and some others are going out." Jessica changed into another top. "Invite your friend Kallyn, too."

Cece thought it over. It would be nice to see Will tonight, even if Jessica was draped all over him. "That sounds great."

A look of shock came over Jess's face. "For real?"

"Yeah. Why do you look so surprised?"

"Well," Jess said, "to tell you the truth, I was beginning to think studying was your favorite pastime."

"Yeah, but a girl also has to have some fun," Cece said, thinking of Alison, who would be so proud of her.

"Great! Go change and get Kallyn. We're leaving in twenty minutes."

Cece left the room and made her way to Kallyn's. She knocked, and a few seconds later, Kallyn answered. She said a quick hello and hurried back to her desk. She was already wearing monkey-print pajamas. "What's up?" Kallyn typed at her laptop.

"Just wanted to see if you'd like to go out with me, Jess, and a few others tonight."

"Yeah?" Kallyn kept typing. "Where?"

"Actually, I don't know," Cece said.

"Um...sounds good," Kallyn said, "but I think I'll stay here."

Cece laughed. "Kallyn, you're not even listening. What are you doing?" She leaned over Kallyn's shoulder and peeked at the screen. The message window read

MISS YOU. MISS YOU MORE. MISS YOU MORE THAN MORE.

"Oh, you're IMing Ryan."

Kallyn quickly covered the screen. "Hey, don't look, okay? It's kinda personal."

Cece stepped back and smiled. "I can see that. You sure you don't want to come?"

"Sorry, Cece, but Ryan got up early to talk to me. It's so hard with the time difference as it is. Maybe next time."

"All right. I'll miss you tonight, but I suppose *Ryan* would miss you more."

"Very funny," Kallyn said, without even bothering to look in her direction. "Have a great time!"

Cece left and went back to her room to change.

While she touched up her makeup, Jess let her know the dress for the evening would be casual, but she refused to tell Cece where they were going. She wanted it to be a "surprise."

Cece put on a simple tank and her cute new jeans that showed off her curves. Then she popped in the earrings she had bought at Macy's. She inspected herself in the mirror. Perfect. They went to the lobby and met up with Lisa and the guys—Dreyfuss, Michael, and Will. Will looked amazing, dressed in a baby blue polo and a pair of vintage washed jeans. Cece smiled as a million butterflies fluttered in her stomach.

"Hey, Cece. I wasn't expecting to see you," Will said, sounding pleasantly surprised.

"Neither was I." Dreyfuss smiled. "Jess, what did you do to get her to come out?"

"Nothing," Jess said nonchalantly. "She just finally

came to her senses." She slung an arm around Will and steered him out the door.

Cece's smile waned, and her confidence about the evening plummeted. *How was she going to have fun tonight?*

The group took two cabs to their destination, and when Cece got out of her taxi, she saw a brightly lit sign outside of a huge building. It read HAO LE DI. Cece tried to translate it. *Good Happy what?* "What is this place?" she asked.

"Beats me," Dreyfuss said.

Lisa grinned. "You'll see." She and Michael followed Jess and Will into the building.

Cece and Dreyfuss looked at each other. They shrugged, then went inside.

The place was at least a few stories high, judging by the escalators. Chinese pop music piped through the large lobby area, where some teens were talking to each other and laughing. Cece took the escalators with the rest of her group to the second floor, where a few clerks waited behind a counter. Jess walked up to a clerk and, after a few minutes, turned to the group.

"Come on, guys," Jess said. Everyone followed her down a hall, and she stopped in front of a door and opened it. "After you, Cece."

Hesitantly, Cece stepped inside a dimly lit room that was about the size of her bedroom at home. But instead of a bed, there was a long U-shaped couch along the wall, a

touch screen at one end of the couch, a coffee table, and a big flat-screen TV.

After everyone was inside, Cece said, "So now can you tell us what we're doing?"

"Isn't it obvious?" Jess sat near the touch screen, and everyone took a seat. "Tonight we're partaking in the fine art of *karaoke*." She tapped at the screen and pulled up a song list.

"Karaoke?" Dreyfuss and Cece said.

"Here?" Dreyfuss glanced around the room. "Like where's the piano bar and the cheesy singers?"

"That's the States," Jess said. "The Chinese are way classier. We can let loose in the privacy of our very own room."

"Wait," Cece said. "I thought karaoke was Japanese."

"It is." Jess reached behind the console and grabbed two microphones. "But that doesn't mean it's not popular here."

Cece stared at the mikes. She wasn't sure she wanted to embarrass herself in front of everyone. Especially Will.

"Don't worry," Lisa said. "This'll be great." She grabbed one of the mikes from Jess. "Jess, why don't you order some drinks, and I'll start us off."

"Good idea." She pressed a button in the console, and when someone answered, she spoke Chinese.

Cece leaned back on the couch as Lisa selected her

song. Cece gave a sideways glance at Will, who looked amused by her discomfort. "The point isn't to sing well, Cece," he assured her. "It's to have fun singing badly."

"Have fun singing badly, huh?" Cece tried to relax and embrace the concept. She took in a breath and smiled. "I guess I can give it a try."

An attendant arrived with a bucket of drinks and a sack loaded with snacks. Dreyfuss reached into the drink bucket, pushed past the bottled water and Coke, and grabbed a beer. "I'm definitely going to need one of these if I'm doing this tonight." He offered one to Cece, who merely shook her head. The last thing she needed was to accidentally overdo it and wind up on the table, dancing and singing bad show tunes.

Jess and Lisa both cracked open their own drinks while Cece peeked into the sack of snacks. She pulled out a bag.

"Shrimp chips," Jess said. "My personal favorite."

Cece cautiously opened the bag and the odor of seafood wafted out. She almost put the bag down, but she told herself she wouldn't let something as innocent as a Chinese snack get the best of her. She popped one into her mouth and crunched the chip. She was surprised to find that she liked it. The taste wasn't nearly as heavy as she thought it would be.

Lisa picked a song. "The trick is to choose songs most people know or it's not nearly as interesting." When the

music for Britney Spears's "...Baby One More Time" came on, the TV played a video while lyrics scrolled across the screen. Everyone groaned, but it was funny to hear Lisa sing it. She wasn't going to win a talent contest anytime soon, yet it was still amusing to see her try to hit the high notes with such a serious expression on her face. Michael was cute, too, attempting to sing along and stumbling over most of the words. Soon Jess was at the mike with Lisa, singing a Madonna song. As the night wore on, everyone got sillier and sillier. Will would sometimes join in with Jess and Lisa, and Cece had to admit, the whole experience was pretty entertaining to watch.

Finally, Lisa thrust the mike into Cece's hand. "Okay, I think it's your turn."

Cece swallowed. "I don't know about this," she said hesitantly. She glanced at Dreyfuss. "Here. Why don't you go."

"Oh, no," he said. "I'm definitely not warmed up enough yet." He held up his beer. "This is only my second one."

"Here, Will," Jess said, holding out the mike. "My throat is getting sore. Show Cece how it's done."

Will took the mike from Jess and sat next to Cece. "Okay, Cece. What do you want to sing?"

"Um..." How was she supposed to sing with Will?!

"Come on, pick a favorite."

"A favorite?" There were so many to choose from. Then suddenly a song popped into her head and she blurted it out. "'You're the One That I Want.' From *Grease*." The minute she said it, she wished she could take it back. Maybe that was too much?

"It's perfect!" Lisa said. "I love that duet."

Will stood and grabbed the mike. "Not to brag, but I'd make an excellent Danny."

"Of course you would, Will." Jess made the selection on the console.

The intro started playing, and Will gripped the mike tighter. Getting into character, he flipped up his collar. Cece, her stomach in knots with nervousness, couldn't help but laugh. She started to feel more comfortable. Will began belting out the lyrics. *"I got chills....They're multiplyin'..."*

Cece giggled. He was so adorable.

Soon it was Cece's turn, and she got into the spirit of things and unleashed her inner Sandy. Jess and Lisa were so surprised, they went into hysterics.

By the end of the song, Dreyfuss was finishing his second beer, Michael looked perplexed but was laughing, and Cece and Will were breathless from hamming it up in front of everyone.

"You were great, Danny," Cece said, returning to the sofa.

He sank down beside her. "No, *Sandy*," he said in his best Danny Zuko voice. *"You were."*

Will held her gaze, and Cece laughed again, and after

a couple of seconds, she thought she saw something genuine flicker in his eyes. "All right, *Sandy and Danny,*" Jess said. "Break it up." She took the mike from Cece. "Michael, it's your turn."

Will cleared his throat and Cece straightened, wondering if she might have imagined the moment.

She looked at Will, and he smiled at her. Maybe not.

The next morning, Cece sent a quick e-mail to Alison.

To: alisofine@e-mail.com
From: cece2me@e-mail.com
Subject: Live from China...

Hey Al,

The last two weeks have been crazy. First the bad news: I'm BURIED with schoolwork, and I think I'm developing a taste for shrimp chips—China's version of seafood Doritos—don't ask.

The good news? I've enlisted Peter, my host in the program, to help me when I go to the orphanage. And some more good news...I had a great time last night singing karaoke with Will—the epitome of perfection. We did a duet from *Grease,* and had so much fun. Of course, it might have been no big deal to him. But seriously, Al, it was the highlight of my night!

—Cece

Smiling, she closed her laptop.

Quickly gathering her things, Cece headed out to the tour bus for the program's excursion to some of Xi'an's most popular landmarks—the Bell Tower, the Drum Tower, and the City Walls.

"So, did you have a good time last night?" Kallyn said as Cece sat down next to her.

Cece nodded, thinking of Will. "It was nice. A bunch of us sang karaoke."

"Oh?" Kallyn lowered her voice. "Was Will there?"

"Uh, Kallyn..." Cece glanced over her shoulder toward the back, where Jess and Will usually sat. "Maybe we shouldn't talk about this now."

"But they're way back there," Kallyn said.

"Well, there's not much to say. We sang, we laughed, I did an impersonation of a blonde desperately in love... that's it."

Kallyn giggled. "I'm sorry I missed it," she said as the bus pulled out of the lot.

Half an hour later, Cece could see the familiar site of the Bell Tower through the window. After everyone got off the bus, they descended underground and walked below the street to get to the tower. When they reemerged, they climbed another staircase to reach the platform where they had a close-up view of the tower. Cece was overwhelmed by the amazing building. The three-story structure looked imposing, with a sloped tiled roof, its four

corners curving upward toward the sky. It was nothing less than spectacular, from the ornate timber beams running across the eaves, to the brightly colored painted columns running upward.

The group gathered outside the building, and Jenny and Mark led the tour. "As many of you know, the Bell Tower is the symbol of Xi'an," Jenny began. "It was built in 1384 during the Ming dynasty. The bronze bell that hung in the tower is now resting over there."

Cece glanced at an enormous bell in one corner of the platform. It was at least twice her height and was suspended above the ground by a wooden frame. A long wooden log was tethered to the frame and hung horizontally beside it, no doubt to ring the bell.

"For over four hundred years, this bell rang every morning to give Xi'an's citizens the time. The bell in the Drum Tower, the building lying to the west, sounded at dusk to signify the end of the day."

"If you want," Mark said, "you can pay ten yuan and ring the bell yourself. Inside the tower, you can have a look at more bells that were used in practice as musical instruments during the same dynasty, and if you go upstairs, you can see the view from the surrounding balcony. This shouldn't take you long, so return here in thirty minutes, and we'll move on to the Drum Tower."

Already some of the students were lining up to ring the bell. "You want to give it a try with me?" Kallyn said.

"Sure. It looks like a great photo op."

They got in line.

"Actually," Cece said, "the view behind us is pretty good, with the City Walls in the background." She dug out her camera from her purse. "Could you get a shot of me while we wait in line?" The giant bell rang as students took their turns.

"No problem." Kallyn took Cece's picture.

"Hey, Cece!"

Cece saw Jessica approaching. Will, Lisa, and Dreyfuss were standing behind her, waiting by the tower entrance. "Let me get one of you and Kallyn," Jess said.

Cece and Kallyn stood together, and Jess snapped the photo.

"Now if you could get one of me and Will..." Jess said, giving her camera to Cece. "Will! Let's take a picture!" Jess turned to Cece. "I don't really care what's in the background. Just make sure you don't chop off my head or anything."

"Uh, sure," Cece said, taking the camera. As Jess and Will stood by the platform's wall, Cece stepped out of line to get the shot. "Okay, guys..."

Jess put an arm around Will.

Cece could barely look at the screen. "On one... two..."

Jess stuck out her leg and held up her arms. Will laughed and grabbed her to keep her balance. *Ugh.*

"Three." Cece snapped the photo, then tried to erase the image from her mind.

"Thanks, C," Jessica said, smiling—or was that a smirk?

"Cece!" Kallyn called. "It's your turn to ring the bell."

Cece returned the camera to Jess. "Hope you like it," she said with as much cheer as she could muster. Then she headed for the bell and stepped up to the timber, chastising herself for getting excited about her tiny non-moment with Will during karaoke. Why did she spend any energy thinking about it when it was clear Jess and Will had a *million* moments together?

Cece paid the attendant ten yuan. She gripped the timber, then swung it as hard as she could. She almost went deaf from the sound.

"You all right?" Kallyn said as Cece stepped down. "You seemed kinda angry up there."

Cece dusted off her hands. "I'm better now."

"It's about Jess and Will, isn't it?" Kallyn said in a low voice as they headed toward the tower entrance. "I saw how Jess was clinging to him for that photo."

"Sort of."

They climbed the steps to the entrance.

"Don't let them get to you," Kallyn said.

"Easier said than done." Cece pushed back her hair. "Anyway, I didn't come to China to obsess over other people's love lives." She changed the subject. "Let's check out the tower."

Kallyn opened the door, and they stepped inside. Instantly Cece's mood improved when she saw three long rows of rectangular-shaped bells, ordered by size, in front of her. She gladly let her mind take her to another place, imagining what it would have been like to live at that time. She could already picture someone, standing before the bells, ringing them to play a song.

Next, Kallyn and Cece went up a narrow staircase to the second floor. There, they found a gift shop selling postcards and touristy knickknacks.

"Perfect!" Kallyn said. "I have to get a postcard for Ryan."

Cece noticed other visitors wandering out to the balcony. "But what about the view?"

Kallyn browsed through a rack. "I'll catch up with you in just one sec."

Cece ventured outside, and the view was terrific, although somewhat hazy. The Bell Tower stood at the center of Xi'an, where four major roads crossed. Traffic circled around the tower, and beyond that, Cece could see all the old and new buildings that made up the cityscape. She could also hear the sound of the bell ringing from the platform below. But what grabbed Cece's attention the most was the instrumental Chinese music coming from a large

public square below. About thirty elderly people in the square practiced tai chi together, moving in slow motion with their arms and legs in a warrior stance.

Cece leaned against the balcony rail, studying them a while longer. Then she looked past the square, at the citizens crowding the streets, the signs written in Chinese, and the bikes, buses, and cars.... It was all so different from everything she knew, and it made her wonder if China would ever feel like a place where she could belong. Like she could be a part of this country, too.

She listened to the bell ring over the city.

Then she saw her purpose here with more clarity than ever before. Who cared what happened with Will and Jess? It was trivial compared to what she was about to embark upon in Beijing in a couple of weeks. She would be getting a chance to learn more about herself, and that was what she should be thinking about.

"Hey," Kallyn said, interrupting Cece's thoughts. "What are you thinking about?"

Cece straightened. "Oh, nothing."

"It didn't look that way to me. Care to share?"

"I was just thinking about...um...my heritage, I guess."

"What do you mean?" Kallyn asked.

"Well..." Cece rested her hands on the rail, then looked at Kallyn briefly before she spoke. "I'm adopted from China, and being here makes me wonder about myself and my past."

"Wow. How old were you when you left?"

"Two."

"Then you really don't remember anything, huh?"

"No, but I hope I can make some sort of connection. I have the address of my orphanage in Beijing, and I thought I'd go there. See what I can learn."

"Really?" Kallyn said. "What do you want to find out?"

"Oh...I don't know." Cece ran a finger along the balcony rail. "Maybe who my birth parents are. Why I was given up. Stuff like that."

"Cece, I had no idea," Kallyn said. "Why didn't you tell me earlier?"

Cece pushed back her hair. "I guess it's sorta weird for me to talk about it. Plus...I'm not exactly going with my parents' blessings. I mean, my dad is okay with it—he thinks I should see where I grew up for two years—but my mom would totally flip."

"What's she worried about?"

"I think she's afraid of what would happen to our relationship if I found my birth mother. But I'm not trying to replace anyone. I only want to know a little more, you know?"

"I can't imagine not knowing who my biological parents are." Kallyn turned to Cece. "You have to let me know if there is anything I can do, okay?

"Sure, Kallyn," Cece replied, smiling. "Thanks."

After everyone was done with the Bell Tower, they

descended below the ground and resurfaced near the Drum Tower, a building similar in design to the Bell Tower. And as at the Bell Tower, students could pound a huge drum with a large mallet for a fee.

By the time they left the Drum Tower, Cece was eager to visit their last destination for the day, the City Walls. The group walked to its south gate, and Cece and Kallyn climbed a wide staircase made from giant blocks of stone until they were almost five stories aboveground. When Cece took the last step, she was impressed not only by the view, which was similar to what she had seen from the Bell Tower, but also by the sheer width of the walls themselves. Two lanes of cars could easily drive here. Cece also noticed that every hundred feet or so, a small building was built into the wall. It wasn't hard for her to imagine soldiers patrolling the walls, protecting the city within, and using the buildings as defense posts. And just to her right atop the wall stood a much larger building with a sloped roof like the Bell Tower. Cece wondered what it was for.

Jenny and Mark gathered the group together once more. "Xi'an's City Walls make up the most complete city fortress that has survived in China," Jenny said. "The perimeter is nearly fourteen kilometers long." She went on to explain how the smaller buildings had been used, and Cece had guessed correctly—as sentry buildings, in which soldiers could protect the wall without exposing themselves to enemy forces. Jenny also pointed out the ramps that were used by military horses, and she said the larger buildings marked the gates to the city.

When Jenny was done with her overview, Mark encouraged everyone to visit the larger building. "That is a gate tower, which served as a defensive outpost. There are three here on the City Walls. The one closest to us now is labeled as a museum, but truthfully it's more like a store where they will try to sell you a jade statue of a winged lion called a *pixiu*. It's worth seeing the mythic-looking creature. The *pixiu* is seen almost everywhere in China and is usually placed in pairs in front of businesses. They have been used for centuries to preserve wealth and fend off evil. The museum has a fairly large example in the lobby. If you donate some money to the *pixiu,* it might bring you some good luck. If that doesn't interest you, you can simply stroll the walls, or, if you prefer more speed, you can rent an electric vehicle or bike over there." He pointed to a makeshift building behind them. "But I have to admit, you might want to save that for another visit when you can come at dusk. The evening lights come on, and the view becomes truly unforgettable. All right, that's it, everyone. Be back at the bus by three."

When the group broke up, Kallyn looked at Cece. "So, what do you want to do?"

"Let's see this *pixiu* Mark was talking about."

Kallyn and Cece walked inside the museum, where a large statue of a winged lion was encased in glass. At the

103

top of the glass was a slot where money could be dropped in, and covering the lion's feet were bills and coins—currency of all kinds: Chinese, German, American...

"It's like a fountain in the States," Kallyn said.

"And they must really believe in it." Cece had already spotted two one-hundred-dollar bills.

"Let's make a wish, Cece." Kallyn dug in her purse and pulled out a dollar bill.

"All right." Cece took out a dollar from her wallet.

Kallyn closed her eyes and held up her money. "Are you ready?"

Cece dangled her bill above the slot and squeezed her eyes shut. "Yup."

"One...two...three."

Okay, lion. I know this is a lot to ask, but please bring me tons of good luck when I go to Beijing. Maybe even help me find my birth parents. No, let's not go overboard here. Just help me find out an answer or two to my questions.

She dropped the money in.

"What did you wish for?" Cece said.

"You're not getting that out of me," Kallyn replied. "It won't come true if I tell you."

"Uh, Kallyn, I'm not sure this is how the lion works."

Kallyn laughed. "You can probably guess it anyway."

Cece nodded. "You wished Ryan and you could live happily ever after, am I right?"

Kallyn blushed. "Maybe...and I bet I know your wish, too."

"Perhaps." Cece said, smiling.

They turned to leave the building.

"Cece," Kallyn said. "I hope your wish comes true."

Cece glanced over her shoulder at the lion. "Me, too."

Chapter Seven

The following Monday, Cece met with Peter over lunch.

"I looked up the address," Peter said the moment they sat down with their food. "It is in the south section of Beijing. Once you get to the city, it will be easy to reach by taxi."

"That's great," Cece said as she started unloading her tray.

"Do you know where S.A.S.S. will be when you are there?"

"I was going to ask Jenny for the schedule today." Cece reached for chopsticks from a glass container on the table. She passed Peter a pair. "She's got office hours this afternoon."

"Good," Peter said. "Once we know, we can plan."

"Exactly. So have you figured out how you're getting to Beijing?"

"I will take the train like everyone else."

"Well then, here." Cece pulled Chinese yuan from her wallet, about 100 U.S. dollars. "I'm paying for your train ticket." She laid the money on the table.

"Xiao Mei!" Peter quickly covered the bills with his hand. "Do not wave money around like it is nothing. You are asking for trouble."

"Oh, sorry!" Cece hadn't been thinking. The amount on the table was easily a week's pay for the average Chinese citizen.

Peter pushed the money toward Cece. "I cannot take this anyway."

"Why not?"

"I am your friend."

"That's ridiculous," Cece said. "You are doing me a favor. It's the least I can do." She put her hand on top of his and pushed it back. "Besides, my mom gave me extra money this summer in case of an emergency. I think this counts as an emergency, don't you?"

"Well..." Peter looked unsure.

"Look, this is how we do it in America. I don't expect you to go around buying train tickets you would have never

bought in the first place if it weren't for me. And besides, you need to save up for when you go to L.A. I insist."

Finally, Peter accepted the money. "Thank you."

"No, Da Ge, thank *you*."

"But if I take this, you must now come to my house for dinner," Peter said. "*I* insist."

"Peter, you don't have to do anything. Seriously."

"No, Cece, this is how we do it in China. You do something, I do something, you do something, I do something. . . . It goes on forever. As does the friendship." He grinned. "Besides, I am not the one who will go to any trouble. My mother is an excellent cook, and my dad loves to talk. I will do practically nothing."

Cece smiled. "Well if it's in the name of Chinese custom, how can I say no?"

"Tomorrow then?"

Cece didn't even have to think it over. "Tomorrow."

Later that afternoon, Cece returned to the dorm and stopped by the counselor's office to see Jenny about the itinerary. When she went inside, she found Jenny working on her computer.

"Jenny?" Cece said.

She looked up from the screen. "Hello, Cece. How may I help you?"

Cece took a seat across from her. "I was, um, wondering if I could get the schedule for our Beijing trip."

"Oh?"

Cece glanced at the floor. "You see, my mom is kind of super-uptight, and...uh...she's really worried about me traveling outside of Xi'an. She wants to know when and where I'll be the whole time I'm there."

Jenny's face clouded over with confusion. "But your mother already contacted me. Did she not get the e-mail I sent?"

"She did?" Cece said. "I mean, yeah, she did." *Of course she did.* "Mom's kind of bad when it comes to computers, and she wanted me to get it from you so I could tell it to her over the phone."

Jenny turned to her computer. "No problem, Cece. I can e-mail you a copy. What is your e-mail address?"

Cece gave it to her, and Jenny brought up a document. She typed some more and clicked her mouse. "It's all done."

"Thanks, Jenny." Cece got up to leave.

"By the way, Cece, I have a favor to ask of you as well. When you see Jessica, could you tell her to stop by my office? I need to give her a message from her parents."

"Sure."

"Thank you, Cece."

"No problem." Cece left the office and headed for her room.

When she walked in, Jessica was hovering over a skirt spread across the surface of her desk. It looked like

she was…sewing? Since when did she turn into Martha Stewart?

"Hey, Jess," Cece said. "I just talked to Jenny in the office, and she says she wants to see you."

Jess didn't look up as she pulled a needle through the skirt. "About what?"

Cece sat down at her desk. "She's got a message from your parents."

"My parents?" Jessica paused, then set down the needle. "Lovely."

After Jess left, Cece worked on an evolution paper due that week. The topic was straightforward: present the arguments for and against the origin of man in Asia versus Africa and draw conclusions. She spent about twenty minutes, typing up an outline and enjoying the silence of the room. But just as she was about to begin her online research, Jessica burst in. "I can't believe this," she said, slamming shut the door.

Cece paused at her laptop and turned to look at her. "What's wrong?"

"Jenny just gave me a lecture about my attendance." Jess placed her hands on her hips. "She says I need to show up more for class and meet with my host, George."

"I thought she had a message from your parents."

"That was the message. Apparently my dad wanted her to check up on me, and she did!"

"So you've been skipping classes?"

110

"Only a few," Jess said, in her defense. "Just the ones that conflict with my personal plans."

"Jess…"

"Mark said that we'd be treated like college students. But apparently not on my dad's watch."

"So don't cut classes then. Meet with George. Problem solved."

"No way, Cece." Jess began pacing the room. "I'm so tired of sitting through all these boring classes that make me want to poke my eyes out. A girl could go insane. And to tell you the truth"—she stopped pacing—"I'm tired of listening to my father. I need a life. *My life.*"

"Is he that bad?"

"Um, yes." She flopped into her chair. "You want to hear a real stereotype about Chinese people? He's a prime example."

"What do you mean?"

"It means that number one, my dad sent me to violin and piano lessons before I turned four.

"Number two, at my age, the words *boys, dating,* and *drinking* are not in my vocabulary.

"Three, if I go to anything but an Ivy League school, I might as well stick the label FAILURE on my forehead.

"Four, when I graduate, I'd better become either a law-yer or a doctor. Or possibly a software engineer—"

"Okay, that's enough," Cece said. "I get the idea." She felt bad for Jess.

111

Then Cece drummed her fingers against the armrests of her chair, wondering if her birth parents would have been like that with her, too. "Why do you suppose your parents are like that?"

"You mean so freakishly anal about everything?"

"Sort of. It sounds like they want you to be a total over-achiever."

"You want to hear my dad's answer?" She did an impersonation. "I don't work so hard to come to U.S. so you play all day. You don't disgrace family like this!"

"So what are you going to do?"

"I don't know..." Jess got up. "Right now, I don't even want to think about it." She grabbed some things from her closet, including a pair of strappy shoes. Then she picked up her purse and headed for the door. "I'll be at Lisa's. Don't wait up for me. I seriously need to go out. *Late.*"

"Jess?"

Jess turned as she opened the door. "Yeah?"

"If you need help with classes or whatever— "

"No, Cece," Jess said. "I'll figure this out on my own."

"You sure?"

"Definitely."

When Cece woke the next morning, she glanced at Jess's bed. It looked exactly like she'd left it the day before. She sighed and got up, trying to put her roommate out of her mind. At least for the time being. Today, she had to finish planning a trip to Beijing.

At lunch, Cece showed Peter the itinerary from Jenny. "This doesn't look good," Cece said.

Peter took the paper from Cece and began to read it.

"I thought there'd be a least one chunk of free time while we're there," Cece continued. "But we leave Friday night, sleep on the train, get to Beijing the next morning, then we're scheduled through ten P.M. And Sunday, we're booked solid from seven in the morning until we take the night train back."

Peter shook his head as he finished reading the schedule. "This can mean only one thing."

"We go to the orphanage really early in the morning or late at night, right?"

"No, who's going to talk to you then?" Peter said.

"Or maybe..." Cece thought about it some more, "we should postpone the trip until I have a free weekend. I think we have one right before our last week."

"Cece, that is a waste of time and money to make another trip when you will already be there. I think this is very simple."

Cece's forehead wrinkled. "It is?"

"You must find a way to depart from this schedule."

"You mean, like, disappear for a while?"

"That is correct." Peter held out the paper. "You see

here on Saturday, you will travel to the Great Wall, which is outside of Beijing, so it will be too hard to leave. Sunday morning, you will travel away again to visit the Peking Man site, but then—this is the good part—you will return to the Forbidden City for the afternoon. That is in the center of Beijing. So Sunday afternoon would be the time to go."

"But how? I can't leave without Jenny and Mark knowing. I'm sure they'll be checking to see we're all together as we move from one place to the next."

"That is what we must figure out. I think you will need to be away for at least three hours to go to the orphanage, stay for a while, and come back."

"I don't know," Cece said. It didn't sound so simple to her. In fact, it sounded pretty risky. What if she got caught?

"We will definitely need more help," Peter said.

"More help?" Cece said. "I've got you, Da Ge. What more could I need?"

"But I am not even supposed to be in Beijing, remember? If you are going to 'disappear,' you will need someone in your program to help you."

Cece immediately thought of Will and Kallyn. Somehow, involving Will, given how much Jess hung around him, didn't seem like the best idea. She'd ask Kallyn. "Peter," she said, "I think that can be arranged."

Later that day, Cece met Kallyn at a café near the university. It was a modern and loungey kind of place, and all around them students studied, surfed the Net, or chatted with their friends on velvet couches.

"So let me get this straight." Kallyn leaned forward in her armchair. "You want me to cover for you while you go to the orphanage."

"Yeah," Cece said.

Kallyn frowned as she clasped a mug of tea. "Oh, I don't know, Cece." She took a sip.

"What?" Cece's heart sank. How could Kallyn say no?

"Of course, I'll do it!" Kallyn said. "Are you kidding me?"

"Man." Cece let out a breath. "You had me there for a second."

"You know, you really are amazing to do something like this. This is so *huge*."

"Don't get too psyched. Remember, I'm not expecting to learn that much. I mean, I'm hopeful, but it's been ages since I was there."

"Oh, Cece," Kallyn said, excitement in her eyes. "I think you *will* learn something. It's like what your dad says. You should see where you grew up for a couple of years. Maybe you'll get your whole life back in a way, versus only knowing what you've known since you've been in the States."

"Yeah…" Cece said. "I guess you're right about that.

Now all we need is a plausible excuse for me to duck out of the program." She took out the schedule and passed it to Kallyn. "You got any ideas?"

Kallyn studied the itinerary. *"Wait a second."*

"Yeah?"

"How come we're not visiting the Olympic Village?"

"Kallyn, focus."

"Oh, sorry." She continued to read the schedule. "I've got it!" She beamed. "Did you see this?" She pointed at the paper. "Looks like we're having a *special* meal at the hotel before we visit the Forbidden City."

"And?"

"Well, we know how you are with certain kinds of Chinese food. I bet there might be an eyeball or two to stare at on your plate."

"Ugh," Cece said, cringing.

"Hey, and you might not even have to fake it! I'd be happy to babysit you at the hotel while the rest of the group heads to the Forbidden City."

Cece smiled. "Kallyn, you are a genius."

Chapter Eight

With Beijing plans in place, Cece was in great spirits when she changed to go to Peter's house that evening for dinner. She hummed to herself as she decided on what to wear. Would jeans be too casual? Should she wear a skirt? She decided on a short-sleeve button-down and paired it with a khaki skirt. It was an outfit any parent would approve of. Pleased, Cece headed out of the dorm to the university gate to meet Peter.

Once they got in a cab, Peter tuned to Cece. "I am excited you will meet my parents."

"So am I," Cece replied.

"And I am thinking," Peter added, "that you should ask my father your question."

"What question?"

"The one about the one-child policy and China's orphans? See what he thinks. He would know much more than me."

"I don't know, Peter," Cece said. "It's so personal." But she had to admit it sounded like a good idea. Perhaps Peter's father could give her more insight on the issue. "Would he really talk to me about it?"

"Yes," Peter said, "my father will talk about anything."

Cece smiled. "I'll think about it."

It wasn't ten minutes more before the taxi let them off. When Cece got out, she noticed the area was similar to that around the university—the streets were lined with restaurants and stores, the sidewalks packed with people. They passed a couple of shops, and Peter stopped in front of one selling DVDs. "This is one of my favorite places." Several patrons were inside browsing the shelves.

"Is this where you get American movies?" Cece asked.

"Yes. I like to call it my research library." He grinned, then led Cece off the main street down a narrow alley. The din of the city quieted as they passed several residential walk-ups. The buildings looked so institutional—basic in design and constructed of concrete. Air-conditioning units jutted out of some of the windows, and laundry hung outside on tiny balconies. Up ahead, a stray dog sniffed at the ground, and from a few of the apartments, Cece could hear people talking.

Peter stopped as they came to a barred security door in one of the buildings. He slipped in a key and pushed it open. The door groaned from age, and Cece followed Peter up a dark stairwell. At each landing, she could see three metal doors with peepholes, presumably leading to apartments. Many of the doors had small bags of trash sitting beside them, waiting to be taken down.

When they got to the third landing, Peter stopped in front of a door, unlocked it, and they stepped inside. *"Ma, Ba!"* Peter called.

The smell of something delicious hit Cece's nose— aromatic and pungent—some sort of meat and garlic maybe? They entered a narrow hall where light spilled from a doorway to the side, and at the end where Cece could see part of a room. Just a beige sofa with lots of cushions. She heard the sound of a cooking vent whirring and a TV blaring in the background. Peter's parents probably hadn't heard them come in.

A line of shoes were by the door, and Peter took his off and gestured at Cece to do the same. Then he handed her a pair of slippers.

Obediently, she removed her sandals and put on the slippers. "Is there a reason why we have to take off our shoes?" Cece asked. "Is it superstition or something?"

Peter laughed. "No, it's because our shoes are dirty.

And besides, slippers are more comfortable anyway."

"So it's not a custom?"

Peter gave Cece a funny look. "Is it a custom in the U.S. to dirty your floors?"

Cece's face warmed. "Point taken."

"Come with me." Peter stepped through the doorway to the side. Cece could now see the inside of a tiny kitchen with plain walls and open shelves instead of cabinets. At one end of the sparse space, a small lady wearing a cotton shirt and slacks stood in front of a wok.

Peter spoke to his mother, and amid the commotion of her cooking, she glanced back, smiling at Cece. She looked so much like Peter, with the same narrow eyes and the sharp nose. *"Ni hao,"* she said. *How are you?*

Cece stammered the phrase back. With only a few weeks of classes under her belt, she wasn't quite comfortable with speaking Chinese outside of school just yet. She hoped Mrs. Lu wouldn't notice how bad her accent was.

Peter's mother nodded, then absentmindedly touched her hair. She spoke rapid-fire Chinese to her son, and Cece caught only a couple of words. *Go. Wait?* Huh? It was much too fast.

"We'd better get out," Peter explained. "My mother is not quite ready. We should wait in the other room."

Cece smiled at Mrs. Lu and left the kitchen, following Peter down the hall. They passed a few closed doors to the right. "Our bathroom and bedrooms," Peter explained.

They reached the room at the end, and a man was sitting in a rickety chair, facing an old TV set. In the corner was a table set up with bowls, saucers, and chopsticks. She guessed that Peter's apartment didn't have a separate dining area. The place was pretty small. As soon as Peter's father saw them, he grinned widely and hurried to turn off the television. Cece noticed that Peter and his dad had the same smile, and for a fleeting moment, she felt envious of the strong features Peter shared with his parents. If only she knew what her birth parents looked like.

"Hello!" Peter's father said. His voice boomed, filling the entire apartment.

Peter introduced Cece. *"Ba, zhe shi Cece."* He turned to her. "Cece, you can call him *Lu Laoshi*. He is a professor at Xi'an Polytechnic."

"Ni hao, Lu Laoshi." Cece said, trying to pronounce each word as confidently as possible.

"I am fine," Lu Laoshi said. "How are you?"

"You speak English?" Cece replied.

"Of course," he said. "I learn in college. Like Peter. It is not so good, but it is good enough."

"My dad is a professor, too," Cece said, happy to have a connection with Peter's father. "He teaches paleontology."

Peter's father looked confused. "Paleontology..."

"Dinosaur bones," Peter explained.

"Ah, I see. I teach *hua xue*, chemistry."

"Wow," Cece replied. Chemistry was one of the hardest

subjects she had ever taken. "I wish my dad taught that. I could have used the help."

Lu Laoshi smiled just as Peter's mother came in, her hair now smoothed into a neat bun. She held a couple of platters loaded with steaming food. She set them on the table. *"Duibuqi, bu hao yisi. Rang ning deng, ah. Qing zuo, qing zuo."*

"Mrs. Lu says she is sorry for the wait." Lu Laoshi gestured at a chair. "Please have a seat."

Cece sat down, and Peter and his father joined her at the table. Before Cece could even study what was laid before her, Peter's mother asked, *"Ning yao he shenme?... Cha, shui, ke kou ke le?"*

This time, Cece got it. Peter's mom was asking what she would like to drink. It was right out of her lessons from the week before. Cece asked for tea, always appropriate for a Chinese meal.

"Please excuse my wife," Lu Laoshi said. "She knows very little English. And she is much too embarrassed to speak it."

"I understand," Cece replied. "My Chinese isn't great either. My brain could explode any minute."

Peter's father laughed.

"But you are doing well," Peter said. "Remember, you have a great tutor, right?"

"Oh, right," Cece said, smiling.

Soon Mrs. Lu returned with tea for everyone, and she

sat at the table, a cheerful expression on her face. *"Women kaishi ba. Qing yong."*

Peter's family picked up their chopsticks. Cece did the same.

Laid before her were two plates of dumplings, but unlike the potstickers Cece had had in the States, these were more delicate and translucent. There was also another platter of roasted beef and egg, and a plate of radishes.

"This is traditional welcome meal," Peter's father said. *"Jiaozi*—dumplings. The rest are cold dishes to eat with dumplings. Please. Try."

Cece aimed her chopsticks at the closest dumpling, but it was one of the slipperiest things ever. Thankfully, she managed to balance one on her chopsticks, and she took a bite. The dumpling burst with warm juices in her mouth. Cece tasted cilantro and steamed pork—delicious!

"This is very good," she said to Mrs. Lu.

"Nali, nali," Mrs. Lu said modestly, which Cece had learned in class was a polite way of saying thank you when given a compliment.

"So Cece, how you like Xi'an?" Lu Laoshi said.

"It's been wonderful so far," Cece replied. She told him about how Peter took them to the Muslim district and her trip to the City Walls. As they talked and ate, Peter translated so Mrs. Lu could keep up. Lu Laoshi asked Cece how her home city in the States compared to Xi'an.

"Well, Dallas is definitely way more spread out than

here," Cece explained. "Mostly, I have to drive everywhere. It's a little hotter, but the people are just as friendly."

Finally, Mrs. Lu spoke up, and Peter translated. "My mom wants to know how your family got to the States."

Lu Laoshi nodded. "I want to know, too."

"Oh," Cece said.

Peter gave her an encouraging look.

Cece twisted the napkin in her hand. "I'm adopted. So I guess you could say my parents just flew me home on a plane."

Peter translated for his mother.

"Ah," she said.

"This trip to China is very special for you then," Lu Laoshi said. "You have come home." He raised his cup of tea toward Cece. "Welcome, welcome."

Cece smiled as everyone raised their tea cups and clinked them. For the first time since she arrived in China, she was beginning to feel at home.

When they set down their cups, Peter caught her eye.

Cece stared at him. "What?"

"Ask my father your question. Now is a good time."

Peter's dad looked at her. "What question, Cece?"

Cece glanced at the table. There were only a few dumplings left. Mrs. Lu was already beginning to clear the dishes. Cece gathered her courage. "Well..."

"Go ahead, Cece," Lu Laoshi said, smiling. "My mind is open book."

Cece took in a breath. "Well, Peter and I were talking about my adoption, and I've been told that many parents here want boys instead of girls. Do you think that's true?"

Lu Laoshi looked thoughtfully at Cece before he answered. At last he said, "You must understand traditional Chinese way of thinking. My own parents are good example. I have three sisters. I am youngest. But I carry family name, yes?"

Cece nodded, though she didn't like where the conversation was heading.

"And when Peter was born, his grandparents very, very happy. We are happy, too, of course. He is our child.

"And for many people here, especially in countryside, if child is girl, grandparents not so happy because the family name does not go on. Older generation has much power in family decision."

"I understand," Cece said. But in all honesty, she didn't. Why didn't the parents just stand up for themselves?

"So yes, I think many girls abandoned for this reason. China knows this is big problem. The government has changed one-child policy. Now if couple's first child is girl, they can try again for boy."

"But doesn't that just mean China's *second* girls are given up?"

"Well..." Lu Laoshi looked uncomfortable. "It is true it will not solve the problem. But it will help. China cannot move too fast or the population will become unmanageable.

125

However, remember this, Cece. Not every parent is the same. I know if my child was a girl, I would not abandon to have boy."

"You wouldn't?" Cece said.

"No."

At this, Cece felt a glimmer of hope.

"Of course, there are people my age who are different. Traditional thinking is still here. It is part of our culture. But it is less and less. Now China has so few girls, it is hard for boys to marry. Many think girls have become more special, and they are treated like queens. Right, Peter?"

"Yes, and they know it, too," he groaned.

"So over time, maybe things will come into balance," Lu Laoshi said. "That's what we hope. Did I answer your question?"

Cece nodded. "Yes, thank you."

"Good." He put his hands together. "Now we have traditional dessert," he said as Mrs. Lu set down a plate of sliced oranges.

As each of them took a slice off the plate, Cece pondered what she had just learned. Though she hadn't completely gotten the answer she had hoped for, she wasn't exactly disappointed, either. Lu Laoshi had said that not everyone was the same, but she hoped that her birth parents might be a lot like them.

Chapter Nine

The next afternoon, Cece got back to her room, reeling from the day's classes. All of her professors had starting talking about midterms, and Professor Hu went on and on about how topics for the final paper would be due in a couple of weeks: "choose wise—forty percent!" To top it off, Cece still had a mountain of work to do that night, which included finishing a paper for archaeology and studying for a language quiz. She tossed her backpack onto her desk and sank into her chair. Then she glanced at Jess's side of the room. Everything was the same as yesterday, except the skirt that had been on Jess's desk

was now hanging from her closet door. That made two days in a row that Cece hadn't seen her roommate. Jess was probably with Lisa. Or hanging out with Will.

Will. When was the last time she daydreamed about him? She pictured him in that cute baby blue polo and sighed.

Cece opened her laptop and worked for a couple of hours to finish her paper, and just as she was about to open her language textbook, someone knocked at the door.

Cece got up, thinking it was probably Kallyn, wanting to hang out.

She opened the door and found Will standing in front of her. Her heart beat faster. "Hey, Will."

"Hey, Cece." He glanced over her shoulder. "Is Jess here?"

"Um, I thought she was with you or Lisa."

"She was with me. But I sorta upset her, and I was hoping she came back here." He sighed. "I'll check with Lisa then." He turned to leave. "Actually, Cece, can I talk to you about this? I could use a girl's opinion."

"Uh…" Cece wasn't sure she wanted to act as counselor for Will and Jess's relationship, but she couldn't exactly say no either. "Sure." She let him in. "So what happened?"

Will sat in Jess's desk chair. "Well…I'm sure it's no surprise to anyone that Jess and I have been hanging out a lot."

"Yeah," Cece said. *Did he have to remind her?*

"And the thing is...well, she was kinda driving me crazy. I mean, like in a bad way."

"Really?" Cece said.

"Yeah. Everywhere I turned, there she was. Look, don't get me wrong, Cece. I'm not knocking your roommate. Jess is a great friend. She's cool. But in doses, you know?"

Cece nodded. "I think I understand."

"Anyway, we were hanging out in my room, and I finally got the nerve to tell her I needed some space. And that's when she got upset and stormed out." Will let out a breath. "So what should I do?"

Cece bit her lip. She was so out of her element. How could she possibly give Will advice about Jess when she totally liked him? "I'd let her calm down first, maybe? You're probably the last person she wants to see now."

"Yeah..." he agreed.

"I'm sure this will work itself out somehow." *That sounded good.*

"All right, Cece. Wait, then talk." Will got up. "Thanks."

"Sure."

He started for the door, then turned back. "I've been meaning to ask...how are things with, uh, Beijing?"

Cece smiled. "Good. I think everything's under control. And your parents?"

"It's been pretty quiet. Dad probably hasn't broken the news yet." He glanced at the door. "Well, I'd better go."

"Right."

But he made no move to leave. He only looked at her for what seemed like a really long time. Finally, he said, "Seriously, if you need anything, let me know."

Cece tucked her hair behind her ear, feeling the weight of his gaze. "Thanks, Will."

Suddenly, the door opened, and Cece and Will turned.

Jessica was standing there, a stunned look on her face. She glanced at Cece, then Will. "I thought *somebody* needed some space. Whatever!"

"Jess—" Will said.

The door closed as quickly as it had opened.

Cece got up. "I'll talk to her."

"Let me go with you."

"No." She opened the door. "I think you'd better stay here."

Before Will could respond, Cece hurried after Jess, who was already near the elevators. "Jess, wait!" She caught up to her.

Jess turned around, glaring. "I have never been so embarrassed!" She pushed the button for the elevator. "If Will and you are hooking up, why didn't you just tell me instead of going behind my back?"

"Jess, we aren't hooking up—"

"Don't try to deny it, Cece." She pressed the button some more. "I knew something was going on since that night at karaoke." She looked toward the ceiling. "I've been so stupid! You've liked him this whole time, haven't you?"

Cece couldn't answer.

The elevator dinged open.

"You know what?" Jess stepped in. "Don't bother telling me. Your silence says it all."

Cece could only stare at her as the doors closed.

That night, Cece met with Kallyn in the student lounge in her dorm. They sat on the couch while Cece relayed what had happened from the moment Will showed up at her door to Jess leaving in the elevator. "So Jess knows you like Will now, huh?" Kallyn said.

"I didn't deny it," Cece replied, "and after she was gone, Will and I decided we'd better just lay off. You should have seen how mad she was."

"And now she thinks you guys have something going on."

"Yup."

"But you kinda do, don't you?"

Cece stiffened. "Excuse me?"

"The way you described how he lingered in your room, how he looked at you just before Jess showed up—that didn't sound like nothing to me. He likes you, Cece."

"He hardly knows me. Maybe he was just being nice."

"*Please. You* like him, and you hardly know him. Are *you* just being nice?"

"No, but…"

"But what?"

"Well, if he likes me so much, why hasn't he asked me out?"

"Uh...what have we just been talking about? He's been with Jess twenty-four/seven since the program started. And if that's not the sole reason, then maybe you haven't given him any idea that *you're* interested. Have you sent out any smoke signals?"

Cece nodded. "I have."

Kallyn raised an eyebrow. "Since when?"

"Um...when I went out to the club. We touched knees. And then during karaoke, I joked around with him."

Kallyn laughed. "Yeah, that's smoke signals. There's your problem. Everyone knows that guys are dumb when it comes to reading girls. And I'm guessing you are about as hard to read as a Chinese textbook. So get out there and start flirting."

Cece shook her head. "Bad idea. Not now."

"Why not?"

"*Jess.*"

"What about her?"

"*Hello,* Kallyn. If I start hitting on Will—if I even knew how—it would make Jess ballistic, and with Beijing barely over a week away, I seriously don't need that right now. I want things calm, peaceful, *sane.* So let's just talk about what I'm supposed to do next about Jess, okay?

"Fine." Kallyn sat forward. "You keep doing nothing."

"Nothing?"

"Well, you certainly won't apologize to her because what would you be apologizing for? And you can't lie to her and say you don't like Will when you already admitted to it, in not so many words. Seriously, aside from escaping the country, you have no other choices. So keep sitting it out. See what happens."

Cece thought it over. "Sit it out, like, *forever*?"

"Yup."

Cece leaned back in her chair. "Okay, at least that's easy."

The next day, Cece went to the theater to meet her project team. As she opened the door, she wondered if Jess would be there. Or if she did show up, would she claw her eyes out or what? When Cece walked in, everyone but her roommate was there, and she felt a little relieved.

"So, Cece, where's Jessica?" Alex said.

Cece shrugged. "Um, I'm not sure."

"I think she'll be here," Will said. "I just talked to her this morning." He gave Cece a reassuring look.

Interesting. Maybe he somehow fixed the situation.

"All right," Alex said. "We'll wait."

Chris kicked his feet up on the chair in front of him. "I'm in no hurry."

Just then, the doors to the theater swung open, and Jess strolled in, looking better than ever. "Hey, everybody."

She came down the aisle and took a seat next to Cece. "So, what topic did we get?

Cece stared at Jess.

"What's up, Cece?" Jess said.

"Um, not much." *What exactly had Will said to her?*

"I checked the board yesterday," Alex said. "We got our number-one choice—the Emperor."

"Excellent." Jess leaned back and studied her finger-nails. It was like nothing had happened the night before. Cece decided she'd have to figure it out later. She turned her attention to the meeting.

"So, I took the liberty of doing some research last night." Alex pulled *A History of China* from his backpack. "I think we need to get acquainted with who Qin Shi Huang really was." He passed the book to Chris, who opened it to a bookmarked page.

"One of the most interesting things I learned," Alex continued, "was that the guy was a total nut."

Chris looked at the book. "And kind of ugly, too." He passed it to Jess, who quickly handed it to Cece. Cece thumbed through the pages and read the headers. "Succession to the Empire," "Achievements and Miles-tones"...

"So what made this guy so whacko?" Chris asked.

"The man was brutal," Alex said. "Killed anyone who got in his way. He amassed a huge army and basically subdued all of the warring states in China. And once he unified China, he began this quest to discover how to live forever. He even started eating mercury, thinking it would make him immortal. Of course, all that did was made him sick and even crazier until he eventually died."

Cece stopped flipping through the book. "That's pretty horrible," she said. "But what does all of that have to do with anthropology?"

That's when Alex leaned in, as if Cece had asked precisely the right question. "Well, you know the Terra Cotta Warriors, the archaeological dig we're going to see next week?"

"Yeah."

"Qin Shi Huang would have never built an army of that scale if he didn't believe in the afterlife in a big way. And if you don't understand what the guy had been thinking, you wouldn't really know what that whole site is about."

"So," Chris said, "what we cover in our documentary is how this man's craziness resulted in the Terra Cotta Warriors?

"Not exactly," Alex replied. "But I think we can find a way to talk about the culture of living in that time period. What people believed then and how the Terra Cotta Warriors are a physical representation of those beliefs."

"I see what you're saying," Will said. "In our film, we

could focus on at least two fields within anthropology: culture and archaeology."

Cece nodded. "Sounds good to me."

"Great," Alex said. "We have a plan. Jess, you agree?"

Jess yawned. "Just tell me what I need to do."

"Okay." Alex pulled out a notepad. "Let's start by divvying up responsibilities...."

The team spent the next couple of hours thinking of everything they would need for a completed project, then assigned roles. They agreed that everyone would participate in the filming. Alex and Chris would be in charge of the script, Cece would work on the subtitles, and Will would take care of the set. Jess volunteered for the costumes.

"So tomorrow," Alex said, wrapping up the meeting, "let's take in as much as we can when we visit the Terra Cotta Warriors. If no one minds, I'll take the video camera first and get footage that we can use in our film later."

No one objected, and they all packed up. Cece put away her notebook and noticed Jess was waiting for her in the aisle. "Let's go, Cece," Jess said.

Cece's forehead wrinkled. Were they back on good terms? She slung her purse onto her shoulder, and they walked out, heading for the dorms.

"Okay, Jess," Cece said, "what's going on? Just yesterday, you acted like you were ready to kill me and Will."

"I know," Jess said. "And I'm sorry about that." She

136

sounded sincere. "I realize you have nothing to do with this."

Cece began to relax. *Thank goodness.*

"I mean, sure, at first I was convinced you were after Will behind my back. But after I stopped to think about it, that's silly. You've been nothing but a friend to me, and with all that studying you do and given all the time I was with Will, how would you have had the opportunity?"

"Right." Cece said, glad that Jess was seeing the truth. Well, most of it anyway.

"Of course, Will found me this morning and tried to explain the same thing. But all that did was solidify what I was thinking already...."

"And what was that?" Cece said.

"That I should be mad at *him,* of course. The guy totally led me on, then tossed me to the street like I didn't matter. What a waste of time! Seriously, just being in the same room with him is torture."

"Okay, but now I'm confused. If you're mad at him, why did you just act like nothing had happened?"

"Well, obviously, we made up. At least that's what he thinks. I told him we shouldn't let anything get in the way of our friendship. Even *space.* Wasn't that big of me?"

"So you're not crushing on him anymore."

"No way. Besides, I'm beginning to think Chris is much more my speed. Did you notice how he looked at me during the meeting? Now that guy has taste."

Cece stopped walking and stared at Jessica.

Unbelievable. The girl could turn her emotions on and off just like that.

"Cece, stop looking at me like that."

"I'm just trying to figure you out, that's all."

"C," Jess continued toward the dorm, "you should know by now that someone like me can't be so easily figured out."

The next morning, Cece had a moment to check her e-mail before she had to meet the group for their excursion to the Terra Cotta Warriors and Horses.

To: cece2me@e-mail.com
From: alisofine@e-mail.com
Subject: Mom alert, Mom alert!

Hey Chica,

I bumped into your mother at the mall. She totally tried to fish some info out of me. She asked if I'd heard from you, saying something like, "Cece must be having too much fun to e-mail her mother. Maybe you've heard from her? I hear she's going to Beijing next week."

I'm not really sure what I said because I was too busy thinking, don't tell her about the orphanage, DON'T TELL HER ABOUT THE ORPHANAGE. I think I blubbered something like, "Have you tried calling?"

She sorta blushed and said she had. So contact her,

please. Your mom is so sweet and I would die if she ever found out I was hiding something from her. I think I won't go to the mall again until you come back. Thanks a lot!
Love,
Al

Cece wrote Alison back, thanking her for keeping up her cover. *Mom had called?* She took the cell from her backpack and realized she never powered it on. No wonder she hadn't known. She filled Alison in on her plans for the orphanage. She also relayed the whole Jess and Will saga. Next, she composed an e-mail to her mother, apologizing for being so hard to reach and explaining it away with details about all of the schoolwork she had to do. This time she ended her message with extra hugs and kisses, but she knew that it wouldn't be enough to keep her mother from worrying. Cece sighed, then grabbed her purse and headed out to meet the group.

She boarded the bus and sat beside Kallyn for the ninety-minute trip out of the city.

"So, what's the deal with Jess?" Kallyn said in a low voice. "I'm surprised that she's even within ten feet of Will."

Cece glanced behind her. Jess was sitting next to Will, but she seemed to be focusing her attention on Chris. "Well, Jess talked to me yesterday, and apparently, she is

trying to be the bigger person by pretending to be Will's friend—don't tell me how weird that sounds—I know. And I've been deemed an innocent party in the whole fiasco. And get this—you see that guy she's talking to? Chris?"

"Yeah. Wait a second, don't tell me. He's the next victim."

"Uh-huh."

"Man, Jessica is something else."

Cece nodded. "Tell me about it."

The bus made its way out of the bustling city, taking a highway into the countryside. From the window, Cece saw miles of flat grassland that looked barely touched, except for the occasional groupings of shacks or signs hinting at civilization nearby. As they drew closer to their destination, the landscape turned into something that resembled suburbia.

Soon, they pulled into a large parking lot, and Cece and Kallyn got off, eager to take in this magnificent place they had seen only in pictures until now. Mark made an announcement to the group. "It will be a long walk from here," he warned. "Xi'an has put a lot of energy into building a commercial area between the lot and the museum. Resist shopping now. We'll give you time to look around afterward." He and Jenny led the group through an area that looked like a fancy outdoor mall. Restaurants and shops flanked both sides of the main pedestrian path, and the path itself was decorated with abstract statues and fountains. In addition to the retail stores, vendors with makeshift tables stood displaying souvenirs, ranging from beautiful paper kites to ubiquitous replicas of the Terra Cotta Warriors.

Once the group arrived at the museum complex, Cece stood before a wide-open square with modern-looking buildings on the left and right, and one larger, domed building in front. Flowers decorated the center of the square. Jenny and Mark stood before the flowers, and Jenny began the tour. "The Terra Cotta Warriors and Horses you are about to see are funerary statues created in 246 B.C. for Qin Shi Huang, the first emperor of unified China. The site was discovered by farmers who were digging a well in 1974. Since its discovery, archaeologists have excavated more than seven thousand warriors, horses, and weapons. We will begin by visiting Pit One, the largest of the three pits open to the public."

Cece and the rest of the group followed Jenny into the domed building. Inside, the space was as large as two football fields. The photos she'd seen didn't do it justice. Cece and Kallyn went up to the railing and looked over. A vast earthen pit lay before them, where rows and rows of statues stood in formation below—warriors, archers, and horses combined. Jenny pointed to a section of the pit marked by a sign. "That is the spot where the farmers tried to dig their well, only to discover broken pottery from Qin Shi Huang's army. What a find, yes?"

Cece nodded. To think all of this was buried for thou-

sands of years and discovered only by chance.

"When you look at the warriors," Jenny said, "note that no warrior is identical. Even the height of the statues varies. Anthropologists theorize that the warriors were patterned after an actual army, or the sculptors were given freedom to exercise their own creativity in the warriors' looks."

Cece turned to Kallyn. "Either way, the craftsmanship is amazing." Some of the statues wore different outfits and had unique hairstyles. Even facial expressions varied from one statue to the next. "I wish I could get closer and touch one," Kallyn said.

Mark stood next to Jenny. "So, you might wonder why the Emperor had this army built. Qin Shi Huang spent much of his days preparing for the afterlife, and while burial objects were common for rulers during that time, no one has seen anything on a scale as large as this. You can also guess the Emperor was something of a megalomaniac. It is also important to note that the army is still fifteen hundred meters away from where Qin Shi Huang's tomb lies. The tomb is believed to contain a palace full of treasure. However, because the burial site is so large, the tomb goes unexcavated. Archaeologists fear there is no way to preserve all of its contents."

"Finally," Jenny added, "scientists estimate nearly seven hundred thousand workers constructed Qin Shi Huang's mausoleum, taking approximately forty years. To keep the location of the tomb a secret, legend says all of those workers, plus the Emperor's concubines, were buried with the Emperor."

Cece grimaced.

"This area has got to be haunted," Kallyn said.

They proceeded to Pit 2 and Pit 3, where more Terra Cotta Warriors had been excavated. The museum had set up glass cases around the pits. Mark and Jenny allowed the group to roam freely and instructed them to meet outside in forty-five minutes. Cece and Kallyn went from case to case, studying each statue. The very last one they approached was the general, the highest rank held in the Terra Cotta Army. Cece observed the detail that went into creating his hairstyle and clothing. She thought she could stand there forever, taking it in. After a few minutes, Kallyn stepped away from the case. "I think I'm ready. You want to go, Cece?"

Cece checked her watch. They still had another five minutes. She wanted to linger a little longer. "I'll be right there."

After Kallyn left, Cece studied the general's face, captivated by his regal expression.

"The general is pretty cool, isn't he?"

Cece turned to see Will standing behind her. Immediately, her stomach fluttered. "Um, yeah."

Will moved to her side and studied the statue some

more. Then he looked around. "So what do you think of this place?"

"It's incredible," she replied quickly, trying to shake off her nervousness. "There's no way our team project will be boring with this as the subject."

"I know.... Actually, I'm surprised by how much I'm enjoying everything so far. Not just the project, but our classes, too."

Cece grinned. "So you're liking anthropology, huh?"

"Who knew studying artifacts could be so cool?"

Cece's stomach fluttered again. Did Will just say the word *artifacts*?

"Anyway," Will said, "I wanted to tell you I'm sorry about, you know, that thing with Jessica. Are you guys okay now?"

"Yeah, thanks for talking to her."

Will smiled. "Good, I'm glad." He looked over his shoulder. "I think the last of the group is leaving. Shall we go?"

Cece nodded.

They headed to the exit, and as Will opened the door for her, she wondered if a perfect guy could become even more perfect.

Chapter Ten

It was Friday. The week had blown by once again. The only difference was Jessica had been staying over at Lisa's every night. Cece didn't mind, though—having the room to herself felt like a perk. She finished packing for the trip to Beijing. She couldn't believe it was almost time to go. In just hours, she'd be on a train with the rest of the students.

Cece opened her wallet, took out the picture, and studied the image of herself as a child. Her stomach twisted with nervousness. She was going back at last...to her home city...where her birth parents could be. She touched

the image and returned the picture to her wallet. Then she zipped up her overnight bag and set it by the door. Now all she had to do was get through a couple more things. First she met with her project team, where they firmed up the script and assigned acting parts to everyone, then afterward, she headed straight to the café near the school to meet with Peter and Kallyn. They went over the details of their plan in Beijing.

"So am I really puking," Cece said, "or am I just making like I'm puking? What did we decide?"

"I think a few gag reflexes are all you need," Kallyn said. "Then I'll stand up and rush you to the restroom."

"Okay. Got it," Cece said.

"So you've got your train ticket, Peter?" Cece said.

Peter nodded. "I arrive late Sunday morning. I will meet you at your hotel room at one thirty p.m."

"Can't wait!" Kallyn rubbed her hands together. "I have a feeling this is going to be really great, Cece."

"Me, too," Peter said.

"I hope so." Cece smiled at her friends and tried to ignore the hammering in her chest.

That evening, the S.A.S.S. group traveled by bus to the Xi'an Railway Station. When they arrived, Cece and Kallyn followed Mark and Jenny across a wide plaza toward a long, imposing building. Outside, locals with their belongings milled around, and inside the scene was the same, only much more crowded.

Mark and Jenny handed out tickets. "These are sleeper trains," Mark told everyone. "Four to a cabin, please." Cece, Kallyn, Jess, and Lisa decided they'd share a compartment. Cece glanced over and noticed that Will, Alex, Chris, and Dreyfuss had formed their own group. After the tickets were distributed, Mark explained how to board the train. "In China, the typical way to get on is to shove your way through, even if you have reserved seating. Don't try to understand the logic. Go with the flow and watch your belongings."

Mark led the group down an escalator to the platform, where more people waited to board. As soon as the train doors opened, it was just as Mark had said—complete madness. Cece and her roomies squeezed onto the train. When they finally burst through the door to a train car, Cece was thankful she and her things had made it in one piece.

It didn't take long for them to find their cabin, a few doors down from the end of the car. The room was compact but very functional. To the left and right were upper and lower berths. In between the berths was a large window, and a short table extended out below it. Cece glanced at a fresh flower that was sitting in a vase on the table. *Nice touch.*

"This almost seems better than the dorm." Kallyn threw her bag onto a sleeper up top. "We even have our own TVs." She gestured at a screen at the foot of her bed.

"Better than the dorm?" Jess said, dumping her things on the lower berth. "I wouldn't go that far."

Lisa sat on the sleeper opposite Jessica. "At least they gave us slippers."

"Well, I think it's like a cute little hotel," Cece said as she took the bed above Lisa.

It was just past eight thirty in the evening when the train rolled out of the station. From the window, the lights of the city whizzed by until the train reached the country-side, and then the view became pitch-black. Cece snug-gled in and faced the wall. But as the train gently rocked, sleep didn't come. Thoughts of her impending weekend started going through her mind. She tried to imagine her visit to the orphanage, but that proved to be difficult. She didn't know what to expect: What would she see? Whom would she meet? Would she be treated with animosity or kindness? And most of all, what would she learn about her birth family? Her thoughts kept circling in her mind, and the harder she tried to sleep, the more awake she felt. By one, Cece had to do something else or she feared she would get no rest at all. Maybe taking a walk would settle her mind. She quietly got out of bed, slipped a T-shirt over her tank top, and redid the tie on her lounge pants. Then she put on her flip-flops and gingerly opened the door.

The dimly lit hall was as quiet as her compartment had been. She moved from one car to the next, sliding the doors open, not paying much attention to where she was headed until she hit a dining car with tables on either side. The food concession was closed, but Cece was surprised to see Will and Alex playing cards at one of the tables.

Will looked up. "Oh, hey, Cece."

Alex turned to face her. "Hey."

"Uh, hi, guys." Cece quickly tried to smooth her hair, then looked down at herself from her T-shirt to her beat-up flip-flops. *Ugh.*

"What are you doing up?" Will said.

"Oh...I...I couldn't sleep."

Alex glanced at Will, then grinned. "Speaking of sleep, I'd better go to bed." He stacked the cards together and shoved them in his pocket. "I'm up by fifty points, Will— don't forget."

He left through the opposite door, leaving Will and Cece completely alone.

Will gestured at the table. "Care to join me?"

Cece wrapped her arms around herself, unsure.

"Come on, Cece. I swear, I won't say anything about the hair." He looked her up and down. "Or the outfit, which is very cute by the way. Grandma pants suit you."

Cece groaned. *"Will."*

"Okay, I won't say any more." He put up two fingers. "Scout's honor."

Already feeling a bit more at ease, Cece headed toward the table. Maybe talking to Will could help. She sat across from him.

"So, how come you can't sleep?"

Cece rested her hands on the edge of the table. "I think it's nerves."

"Nerves?" Will studied her face intently. "Does this have something to do with your birth parents?"

She sighed. "It has *everything* to do with my birth parents. This is the big weekend. I'm going to my orphanage."

"You are?" Will said. "That's great. Wait a second—how? Aren't you going to be with us the whole weekend? Did you get permission from Jenny?"

"Um...no." Cece bit her lip. "And maybe that's part of the reason for the nerves, too. It's kinda complicated."

Will nodded. "Explain."

"Well..." Cece took in a breath, then filled Will in on her plans for the orphanage, including Peter and Kallyn's participation. And as she unloaded it all to him, the weight on her shoulders started to lift. Having Will sit quietly and listen somehow helped her organize her thoughts. But when she got to the part about all of her doubts and questions at the orphanage, her nervousness came back again. "I just can't stop thinking about what's going to happen."

"I think I know what can help," Will said.

"What?"

"Realize what you don't have control over, Cece. All you can do now is hope for the best."

Cece looked at Will thoughtfully. "You're speaking from experience, aren't you?

"Maybe."

"Is that how come you're not totally bent out of shape about your parents?"

Will ran a hand through his hair. "Don't get me wrong, I'm not thrilled about it...but"—he looked up at her and smiled—"it's how I get through it."

Cece drummed her fingers on the table. "Hope for the best? Forget everything else."

"Yeah."

"I guess it's something I could try."

Will got up. "And I think I know something else that might help. Stand up."

Cece stood, wondering where they would go next. But before she could figure that out, Will put his arms around her and gave her a hug. "How's that?"

Cece stiffened, then relaxed in his arms, overcome by his warmth. She rested her head on his shoulder. There was something wonderfully innocent about the embrace. No awkwardness. No pressure. Just someone who cared. About her.

"Yeah," Cece said. "That works, too."

• • •

Cece woke the next morning with the memory of Will's hug lingering in her mind. Then as the train pulled into Beijing, the feeling was replaced by the excitement of seeing her orphanage city. She got off the train with Kallyn and followed the group through a massive train station bursting with life. When they made it outside, Cece noticed the city resembled Xi'an in many respects. New buildings, construction everywhere, lots of traffic. Bicycles. But things here seemed bigger and better somehow. Were the streets cleaner? The architecture more refined? Cece couldn't quite exactly explain it, but the city felt like it was important and official, living up to its role as China's capital.

On the bus ride to the hotel, Cece and Kallyn got a chance to see more of Beijing. "Now, our hotel," Mark explained, "is centrally located near the Forbidden City. And in case anyone is wondering, the palace got its name because no one was allowed to enter or leave without permission from the Emperor. Not surprisingly, the place is also surrounded by a wall and a moat, so we won't be able to get a good view of it when we drive by. However, Tiananmen Square, another major landmark, will be readily visible."

Readily visible was an understatement. Not long after Mark spoke, Cece saw the square through her window—a flat stretch of concrete that seemed to span forever.

"Tiananmen Square," Jenny said, "is the largest of its

kind in the world. It covers four hundred thousand square meters. Over one million people can assemble here for ceremonies, parades, and political speeches."

One million?

"Tomorrow, after we visit Zhoukoudian, the site where the Peking Man was found, we will return to the Forbidden City and see the highlights of the square."

"Hey," Kallyn said, "isn't this the place where all those students died protesting the government?"

Cece nodded. From what she knew from her history class, thousands of students gathered in the square, calling out for democratic reform, and refused to leave. After several months, the Chinese government sent in military tanks, literally crushing hundreds of protestors. It made Cece uncomfortable to think about it.

"You know what I heard?" Kallyn said. "If you Google 'Tiananmen Square' in China, you get no results. Sorta creepy, isn't it?"

"Yeah," Cece said. "I've heard that, too." It wasn't exactly the most appealing story she'd heard about China. Censoring history and killing people who were only expressing their political views ranked right up there. As far as Cece knew, one of the goals of communism was to eliminate oppression. But it seemed to Cece that preventing freedom of speech *was* oppression. Like the government's family policies, it was another of those issues Cece didn't quite understand.

As the bus continued, Mark made another announcement. "We're getting close to the hotel. Now ideally, the program would have liked to set up your stay at a traditional courtyard hotel with Chinese decor, but because those places aren't large enough for our group, we're staying at a Western chain. Once you all have had a chance to check out your rooms, head downstairs for breakfast, and then we'll head out again to the Great Wall. Your bags will be in your room when we return."

The bus pulled up to a modern building about eight stories high. Red carpet covered the entrance floor, and men in uniforms with brass luggage carts awaited them. The canopy above read Holiday Inn.

"This is a Holiday Inn?" Kallyn said. "You'd think this is a Four Seasons."

"I'm not complaining," Cece said, standing up.

They entered the lobby, and Jenny handed out room keys. Cece and Kallyn found their room on the seventh floor, and Kallyn slipped the key into the card reader. The light flashed green, and they stepped inside.

The room was large, complete with two double beds and a sitting area. "Forget the train," Kallyn said, flopping onto one of the fluffy beds. "*This* is way better than the dorm." She grabbed a room-service menu and thumbed through it while Cece went over to the window.

Cece scanned the city skyline. Somewhere out there was her orphanage.

"So what's it like to be home?" Kallyn said.

"Home?"

"You know. Back here."

"Well…" Cece considered Kallyn's question as she examined the view again. "This doesn't feel all that different from Xi'an. I'm beginning to wonder if China will ever feel familiar."

Kallyn got up and looked out the window with Cece. "That'll probably change. Once you get to the orphanage."

"Maybe," Cece said.

"Come on." Kallyn moved away from the window. "Let's go downstairs and meet the group."

After breakfast, the group got on the bus for their excursion to the Great Wall. Jenny explained they would travel about seventy-five kilometers northwest of the city and drive into the Tianshou Mountains, where the Wall crested its ridges. As the bus traveled along a multilane expressway, they left the city behind and entered a beautiful countryside with craggy mountains in the background. The only thing spoiling the atmosphere was the gray sky.

Eventually, it started to drizzle, and Kallyn groaned. "Of all days for it to rain."

"I know," Cece said as she watched the clouds gather. But it wasn't long before the sight of the Great Wall distracted them from the weather. The Wall snaked along the ridge of the mountains, like a long, white dragon stretched atop the misty peaks. It had watchtowers like

the City Walls in Xi'an. But unlike the City Walls, which were flat and in the middle of a burgeoning city, the Great Wall sloped up and down, and everything around it looked untouched. No buildings, no signs, no roads. So majestic and timeless. It was simply beautiful.

"I'm going to climb that bad boy," Kallyn said. "All the way to the top. You want to do it with me?"

Cece nodded. "I'm up for it."

Mark picked up the microphone and addressed the group as the bus made its way toward the Wall. "Due to the rain, I have good news and bad news. The good news is the crowds may be a bit thinned out, which should make your climb more enjoyable. The bad news is we're going to have to cut our trip short if it pours. So if anyone has big dreams of going to the top, it may not happen...."

A collective sigh could be heard throughout the bus. Cece glanced at Kallyn, who looked disappointed.

"If it does rain hard, you will need to slowly make your way down and board the bus. I don't want any serious accidents on the Wall today. Oh, and if you need an umbrella, vendors outside the entrance will be more than happy to sell you one. You'll have two and a half hours to explore the Wall. Afterward, we'll grab some lunch at a local restaurant and walk around the area."

Jenny immediately launched into her overview. "The beginning of the Great Wall dates back to the Warring States period, around 443 to 221 B.C., when the various states each erected walls to defend their territory. Emperor Qin Shi Huang defeated these states and reconfigured the walls to accommodate the new empire—what we now consider to be China."

Jenny went on to explain that through the dynasties thereafter, the Wall was modified as the defensive needs of China changed. The section they would be visiting now had been constructed during the Ming dynasty, a time when the largest efforts on the Wall were made to protect the country from nomadic warriors.

"When you climb the wall," Jenny went on, "you will notice many watchtowers. Soldiers were posted there and would communicate to the Forbidden City in Beijing. They used smoke signals in the event of trouble. It is said the number of smoke signals indicated the size of the invading forces. One signal for one hundred men, two signals for five hundred men, and three smokes for a thousand or more. So when you think of the Great Wall, you may view it as a deterrent and a communication system, rather than a place where battles were fought. Few men were needed to man the Great Wall." As Jenny finished, the bus pulled into the parking lot.

Kallyn and Cece got off, hurried toward the first vendor they saw, and bought umbrellas.

"Are you ready?" Kallyn shouldered a small backpack and popped open her umbrella.

Cece looked up at the Wall. Already tourists were

climbing a chain of steps that seemed to stretch forever, hill after hill, ascending the mountain. It hadn't looked that hard when she had seen the Wall from a distance on the bus. But now, up close, the steepness of it all caught her off guard. She swallowed as she held her umbrella over her head. "Yeah, I'm ready."

"Pace yourself," Kallyn said as they made their way up the wet steps. "You don't want to wear yourself out before we reach the first tower."

Kallyn and Cece steadily made the climb.

Somewhere along the way to the first tower, Cece heard Jessica not far behind her. "Chris, you think you might be able to walk a little closer or something, in case I fall? I didn't wear the right shoes...."

Cece glanced back, wondering where Will was. Among the umbrellas, she saw him not that far behind Jess, climbing with Alex. He caught her eye and smiled.

Cece smiled back, then pressed forward with Kallyn.

Soon they reached the first watchtower, where many people had decided to take a break. Kallyn and Cece kept pushing though, hoping to beat the rain.

As they continued upward, the steps became much steeper, and the path narrowed. Even though Cece wasn't afraid of heights, she was starting to get a bit dizzy. Cece looked back, gripping a handrail, and hoped to see a terrific view, but the cloudy weather made it hard to see much. She hoped the journey would be worth it.

Once they reached the second tower, Cece and Kallyn rested briefly, then higher and higher they climbed, the gap between them and the rest of the students widening. After about forty-five minutes, the rain stopped. Cece could see only a smattering of people ahead of them. Will and Alex were at least a tower behind. She caught her breath and looked up, unable to see where the stairs ended. "Kallyn, can we make it all the way?"

Kallyn took out a water bottle from her bag. She passed it to Cece, then got another bottle for herself. "Absolutely. You see that old lady?" She pointed to a lone woman who was coming down, high above them. "If she can do it, so can you."

Cece nodded and chugged some water.

"Hey," Kallyn said. "Go in front of me. That way you won't be tempted to slow down."

Cece did as she was told, and they climbed higher. It began to feel like she wasn't visiting some tourist destination anymore. This was a crazy test of her endurance, even her courage, as the steps became steeper and narrower. Kallyn seemed to be enjoying every second of it. "Just think how good you'll feel when we make it to the top, Cece."

Just how good will *it feel when I get to the top?* Cece thought. This was one of the hardest things she had ever done. It quickly became a game for her. If she could climb to the highest point of this section of the Great Wall, she could do anything. Tomorrow's trip to the orphanage

would seem like nothing. Her eyes focused on every step she took. She started counting them off. After another twenty minutes, her thighs felt like they were on fire.

"We're almost there," Kallyn said.

Cece looked up again. They really were getting close. Only two more towers. She gritted her teeth. She could do this. She *had* to do this. Higher and higher, she went. The sky darkened once more, and it started to rain.

They moved faster. The rain came down harder, and Cece knew Mark would want them to turn back.

"Oh, we're almost there," Kallyn said.

They didn't even bother to open their umbrellas. It took every ounce of Cece's energy to push forward.

Other tourists who had already made it were coming back down.

Finally, Cece was only steps from the last tower. Now it was raining so hard she could barely see ahead of her. Her hair and her clothes were soaked. But she had just five steps left. *Four...* Her body filled with anticipation. *Three... two...*

She took the last step, and relief washed over her. She thought she would collapse as she stood at the final watch-tower. No one was there. It was as though she was the only person on the planet who had reached the very top.

Cece looked all around her. She had a 360-degree view of the vast expanse of China below. She hadn't even real-ized they had made it above a thin layer of clouds. The clouds rolled across the horizon, allowing the ridges of the Tianshou Mountains to peek through. She felt like she was literally on top of the world.

She stood before the tower, with her arms up to the rain. "We did it, Kallyn!"

Kallyn joined her, surveying the surrounding landscape. "It's totally stunning."

Cece squinted at the sky as the cool rain pelted her face. "You were right, Kallyn. I feel incredible."

"Cece, you couldn't look happier than you do now. We've got to take a picture."

Kallyn opened her umbrella and grabbed her camera from her backpack. She snapped a shot of Cece, then Cece got one of Kallyn. Afterward, they stood together under the umbrella and gazed downward in the direction they had come. Through the rain and mist, Cece could see the stairs below snaking in and out of the clouds. They must have covered at least a couple of miles of steps, if not more.

"So, Cece," Kallyn said, "are you ready for tomorrow?"

Cece looked at Kallyn, still in disbelief that they had made it to the top. Maybe she really could do anything she set her mind to. Maybe China was showing her that she did belong here in some way. *Maybe...* Cece took in the view once more...tomorrow would prove to be amazing, like today.

Cece grinned at Kallyn. "Actually? I think I am."

Chapter Eleven

The next morning, Cece lay in bed, staring at the ceiling. "I can't feel my legs," she moaned to Kallyn.

Kallyn grumbled in her sleep.

"*Kallyn,* I can't move."

"What?" she said.

Cece looked over.

Kallyn was rubbing her eyes. "You're probably just a little sore." She slowly sat up.

"A *little* sore? I'm going to need a wheelchair to get to the orphanage."

"*Please.* Today's your big day. Are you sure you aren't making excuses?"

Cece turned on her side. Yes, she was making excuses. When she had woken up, the first thing she did was worry about all the things that could go wrong today. Forget Will's advice on the train—it was all doom, doom, and doom. What if Peter forgot to show up? Or what if they got lost on the way to the orphanage? Or what if no one would even let them in if they did find the place? She was practically nauseated. "But my legs really do hurt."

"What happened to your enthusiasm from yesterday?" Kallyn said, getting out of bed.

"Gone," Cece complained. "Completely gone."

"Come on." Kallyn came over and pulled Cece into a sitting position. "Rise and shine. I'm not going to hear this anymore."

Cece groaned. She set her feet on the carpet and got out of bed.

It wasn't long before they headed out of Beijing for a short trip southwest of the city to visit Zhoukoudian. Jenny explained the site was a series of caves where the largest samples of *Homo erectus* had ever been found, including a skull of the Peking Man, which was once recognized as proof of the theory of evolution. Once they arrived, however, Cece could hardly focus on what Jenny was saying. She was too busy mentally rehearsing how she would interact

with the people at the orphanage. She'd have Peter introduce her as a former orphan. She'd tell them she'd always wanted to see where she'd spent her first two years. Then she'd ask for a tour like her father had suggested and get to know the care workers a bit. Finally, when everyone was comfortable with her, she'd say, "So... um... do any of you know why I was abandoned?" That's when the room would go silent. No one would have any idea. She'd ask, "Well, perhaps you can tell me where my parents are?" At this point the care workers would gape at her in horror, kick her out, and tell her to never come back.

This was how it played in her head, over and over again, as Jenny walked everyone through the caves. By the time the group finished and returned to the hotel, Cece's doubts had only grown worse. She sat at the table for their "special" lunch at the hotel's restaurant, where she became convinced nothing even remotely disgusting would be served.

Kallyn nudged Cece. "Hey, you've had a permanent wrinkle in your forehead since you woke up this morning. Try to relax, okay?"

Cece whispered in her ear. "I don't think I can go through with this."

Kallyn whispered back. "Yes, you can."

Jess and Lisa joined them at the table, followed by Chris, Dreyfuss, Alex, and Will.

Will took a seat next to her. "Hey, Cece."

Cece gave him a weak smile, then realized she was so nervous that the act of his sitting beside her had absolutely no incremental impact on her heart rate, sweatiness, or body temperature.

"You know, you don't look so hot," Will remarked. He glanced at Kallyn. "Kallyn, what do you think?"

Ugh. She really didn't feel good. She knew Will was trying to help, but at that moment, she wanted to stop the whole thing. She put a hand on her stomach.

Kallyn studied Cece up and down. "Will, I think you're right," she said loudly. "Cece, is something wrong?"

Cece tried to find her voice. "Kallyn, I think..."

"What is it, Cece?"

Just then, the servers started bringing out the food. One laid down a giant fish with bulging eyes and its jaw gaping open.

Oh, man. "I think..." She put a hand over her mouth. "I'm going to throw up."

Everyone pushed back from the table.

Kallyn stood. "Hold on. I'll get you to the bathroom."

Will got up, too. "Let me help."

Cece took deep breaths. She didn't want a repeat of her first night in Xi'an.

"I've got her," Kallyn said quickly. "Will, why don't you get Jenny instead?" She threw an arm around Cece and steadied her as she walked her out of the dining room.

As soon as they got to the hotel's restroom, Cece's head

began to clear. It was good to be away from all the noise, the people, the food. She sat in a chair in the lounge area.

"Man, you're good," Kallyn said. "Seriously, you could have won an Oscar."

Cece rested her head against the wall. "Unfortunately, I wasn't really acting."

"Really?"

She closed her eyes. "But I'm better now."

"Cece, if it's that bad we really need to get you upstairs."

Just then Jenny walked in. "Are you all right, Cece? Will said you might be sick." She looked at Cece with concern. "Do you need a doctor?"

"No," Cece replied, opening her eyes. "I just...um... have a weak stomach when it comes to...Chinese delicacies."

Jenny felt Cece's forehead. "It is no trouble to take you to a doctor. Are you sure you don't want to go?"

"Positive."

"Then let's take you to your room for now, okay?"

"I'll help," Kallyn volunteered.

Jenny and Kallyn got Cece up to her room and in bed. Kallyn brought her a glass of water.

"I will talk to Mark and see if I can stay with you," Jenny said. "Though I'm not sure how he will run the tour without me—"

"You don't have to do that," Cece said. "I just need to rest. That's all." She took a sip from the glass.

"I would feel better if you were not alone."

"Hey, Jenny," Kallyn said. "Why don't I stay with her? We'll just hang out here until the group comes back."

Jenny considered this for a moment. "But don't you want to see the Forbidden City?"

"I've already been there. I saw it last year with my mom," Kallyn said.

Cece looked at her and raised a brow.

"If anything comes up," Kallyn continued, "I can call you."

"Well..."

"Really. It's okay," Kallyn said.

Jenny thought it over.

"All right then," she said, reluctantly. She wrote on a notepad and handed a phone number to Kallyn. "The group will be back at seven. Then we'll go to the train station." She got up and made for the door. "Cece, I hope you feel better. Kallyn, thank you."

After Jenny left, Kallyn leaned against the door. "I thought she'd never leave. What time is Peter coming?"

Cece glanced at the clock. It was one ten. "We've got twenty minutes. But you don't really think I should go through with this now, do you?"

"Um, yeah," Kallyn said.

"But I think I might really be sick."

"Cece."

"All right, all right." Cece pushed back the covers and headed to the bathroom to freshen up.

When Peter arrived at the hotel, Cece met him downstairs, and they got into a cab. Peter gave the driver the address and soon they were off. Peter turned to her. "Are you ready, Cece?"

"Not really," Cece said. "I'm too nervous."

"Then you must find your focus, Xiao Mei."

"I don't think I can, Peter. My focus is completely shot."

"Maybe you need something to remind yourself why you are doing this. Take out your photograph."

Cece pulled her wallet from her purse, then took the picture out. "Here."

"No," Peter said. "You keep it. I want you to look at it, Cece."

"Okay..." Cece stared at the image.

"Now do you remember why we are here?"

"I remember."

"No, think harder. Why have you come all this way?"

Cece looked at the picture. "I'm here to find out why I was given up for adoption."

"And?" Peter said.

"And..." Cece glanced at her parents in the photo. "I want to know who my birth parents are, too."

"And?"

This time, Cece studied the girl, her innocent face...

like before, she wished she could connect with her. "And I guess I'm tired of not knowing who I am."

She took in a breath. She hadn't expected to say that. It was almost painful to think of it that way. But wasn't that what she wanted in the end?

"Cece," Peter said, "are you more focused now?"

"Yeah." Cece sighed and put the photo away. "A little."

"Good." Peter smiled. "That's what Da Ge is for."

Soon, the taxi pulled up to the curb.

"This must be it," Peter said.

Cece looked out her window. Suddenly, what little calm she had felt all but evaporated. "No, this can't be right." All around her were high-rises. It looked like a business district, with company names and logos marking the buildings. Where were the cobblestone walk and the concrete building from the picture? "Peter, do something."

Peter checked the address again with the driver.

The driver sounded agitated, but he didn't move the car.

"No, Cece, this is it," Peter said. "We need to get out. The taxi is blocking the road."

Cece paid the driver and opened the door. "This has to be a mistake though, Peter."

They got out of the cab and stood on the sidewalk. "He says this is the building." Peter pointed at a fifteen-story high-rise that couldn't have been more than a few years old. "The address is correct."

"But..."

Then Cece realized what had happened. "Oh, no, Peter. The orphanage must have been torn down."

Peter stepped closer to the building. He read the directory by the door. "No, Cece, I think it is still here. There is a children's welfare center on the fifth floor."

"That isn't the same." Cece gestured at the new roads and the shiny buildings. "Where I grew up is gone.... It's like everything has been erased." Tears began to well up in her eyes. "It's like a part of *me* has been erased."

"You cannot think that way," Peter said. "I know this is not what you expected, but we should go in and see what we learn, okay?"

Cece wiped at her face. "I don't know, Peter."

Peter gently pulled her toward the building. "You just follow me. I will see what I can find out."

Cece nodded, letting Peter lead her inside.

They took the elevator to the fifth floor and entered a hall where they found the door to the orphanage. Cece pushed back her hair and tugged at her shirt, trying to get herself back together again.

"Are you ready?" Peter said.

Cece took in a breath. "Yeah."

Peter pressed the buzzer.

A young woman opened the door. Peter talked to her in Chinese, and the woman's face brightened. Cece tried to understand what they were saying, but, like her visit to

Peter's house, the pace was much too fast. She could pick up only a word here and there. Finally, the lady asked them to come in.

They stepped inside, and right away, Cece was taken aback by what she saw. She hadn't expected to see something that looked like a day-care center in the middle of a high-rise. But here, toddlers ran freely and plastic toys were everywhere. Different rooms branched from the lobby, where Cece could see small beds and children playing with staff.

Several care workers, holding the hands of young children, came in to look curiously at Peter and Cece. While Peter spoke to them, Cece studied the children's faces. They looked healthy and happy, interested to know who Cece and Peter were. Cece was surprised. Somehow she imagined the kids would be sullen and unkempt. But it was obvious they were well cared for and loved. Cece wondered if she had been treated as well when she was an orphan.

Peter turned to Cece. "One of the care workers will get the director."

Cece nodded.

Soon a formally dressed woman walked in and talked to Peter. As Peter replied, the expression on the director's face became stern. Cece heard, *"Bu xing."* She knew what that meant: *That's not okay.*

"What's wrong, Peter?" Cece asked.

"Stay here," Peter said.

The next thing Cece knew, Peter and the director were walking out of the center. "Peter?"

He shook his head as if to quiet Cece, then closed the door behind him.

The care workers and the kids were still staring at Cece. Some of the children began talking to one another. Then one of the kids spoke to her. Her voice was cute. *"Ni shi shei?"*

Who am I? Cece cleared her throat, "Uh...*wo jiao Cece.*"

The children began talking to one another once more and giggled as though Cece had just said the funniest thing. Cece blushed.

The door opened again, and Peter and the director returned.

"Everything is okay, Cece," Peter said. "The director is happy to have her administrator give you a tour. Afterward, the director will try to answer any questions you might have."

Cece looked at the director, who smiled, and she wondered what Peter had done to make the director change her mind. But she knew now was not the time to ask.

The director left the room, and moments later, a young lady, holding a clipboard, introduced herself. "Hello, I am Chang Hui." Her accent was heavy. "Excuse me, Cece?" she said. "My English not so good. Okay I talk to your friend?"

"That's fine," Cece said.

Chang Hui turned to Peter and began speaking.

Peter translated. "She says the orphanage was taken down only a couple of years ago. Now it is reestablished here."

Chang Hui took them to a large playroom, where kids between the ages of two and four were running about. As soon as the children saw Cece and Peter, many of them gathered around like the others had done. They began speaking animatedly in Chinese. This time Cece only partly understood them. They wanted her to do something, but she didn't know what. "What are they saying?" Cece asked.

"They want you to play a game with them," Peter said. "Pretend games. You can be the princess."

Princess? The idea that these kids wanted to play make-believe with her made her heart warm. Then she noticed something about them that gave her pause.

"Peter, everyone here is a girl," she whispered.

Chang Hui had heard her. "Yes, we have many girls," she said proudly. "Only three boys."

"Cece?" Peter said. "Are you all right?"

Cece forced a smile, and they continued the tour. But as they moved from one room to the next, she kept thinking about what her father had said about the one-child policy. Girls given up in favor of boys.

No, that can't be true for everyone, Cece reminded herself.

They went through the preschool room, the cafeteria, and the sleeping rooms for the older children. The last stop was the nursery, where row after row of cribs had been lined up. Cece refocused her thoughts on what Peter was saying.

"Chang Hui says the most seasoned workers care for the babies," Peter said. "They are assigned to only two infants at a time, so everyone receives proper attention." Indeed, there were about fifteen staff members in their forties and fifties here, holding, rocking, singing to the little ones. "Many of the workers have been here since the orphanage opened in 1980," he went on. "Around the time when China first allowed foreign adoption."

"So it's possible," Cece said, "that someone here may have taken care of me?"

"Yes," Peter said, smiling.

Cece scanned the room on the slim chance that some-one might seem familiar to her, but nothing roused her memory. "Maybe we can ask the director if someone here knows me."

Peter nodded. "We will."

Chang Hui finished the tour and led them back to the director's office. Along the way, a staff member asked Chang Hui a question. As she answered, Cece whispered to Peter, "What did you talk to the director about earlier?"

"She was upset that we hadn't made an appointment.

She told me an orphanage visit must be planned, and it costs money. So I let my money talk."

"You bribed her?"

"Bribe is not the right word, Cece. This is how you must sometimes do business in China. I scratch your back—"

"You scratch mine. I get it. Well, don't worry, I'll pay you back."

"Okay, but you'll have to come to dinner again."

Cece rolled her eyes. *"Peter."*

They neared the office, and Chang Hui opened the door.

The director looked pleased to see Peter and Cece again. They took a seat in front of her desk. Then Cece let Peter lead the conversation as she tried to pick up bits and pieces of what they were saying. Eventually, she decided it was pointless. All she could understand was her name over and over again. So she gave up, her head hurting from concentrating so hard. Finally, Peter turned to Cece and asked her for her Chinese name, her birth date, her parent's names, and when she had been adopted.

Cece took this as a good sign and relayed the information.

The director spoke some more, and Peter stopped the conversation to catch Cece up.

"Cece, there is good news."

Cece straightened. "There is?"

"The director says she can find out who your care worker was. She can obtain the information from your health records. They are archived in the central office, so it might take a few weeks. I have already given her my address and phone number."

"That's great, Peter."

"She also said she can provide you with your finding record. The record contains information about where you were found, your age at the time, your weight. Things like that."

Cece felt a tiny shred of hope light up inside her. "Would it say something about my birth parents?"

Peter spoke to the director some more.

She replied, and Peter translated.

"I guess that is the bad news," Peter said. "She says the parents of orphaned children in China are rarely identified to the state, and for a good reason. It is illegal to abandon a child, so those who do it make sure they're not caught."

"So I won't find out."

Peter spoke with the director again.

"She said it was very unlikely. She has never seen that information for any of her children."

Upon hearing this, Cece felt like a door to a part of her life had just been shut. She knew she wasn't supposed to have expectations about finding her birth parents, but she hadn't planned on someone saying that finding them would be next to impossible.

"Are you okay?" Peter said.

"Yeah, I'm fine." *Keep it together, Cece.*

"Do you want me to ask about anything else?"

Cece could hardly think. "No. Can we go, Peter?"

After the meeting concluded, Cece and Peter stepped out of the office, only to find a few staff members, including Chang Hui, hovering outside as if they had been listening in. Chang Hui whispered to Peter. "Come with me. I try to help."

Cece held her breath. They followed her to the nursery and watched her close the door. She gathered the care workers together.

"She's telling them what she heard in the office," Peter said. "Cece, give her your photograph."

Cece quickly pulled it out of her wallet.

Each of the staff members studied the picture, then eventually one stepped forward. Her face was weathered and kind, and she was taking a particular interest in the birthmark on Cece's face. She glanced at the picture again. *"Ying-Ying."*

"Ying-Ying?" Cece repeated. "What's that?"

"It's a name," Peter said. "Like a nickname."

"*My* nickname?" He heart raced. "She knows me?"

Peter nodded. "I think so."

The woman spoke slowly to Cece, introducing herself. *"Wo shi Wang Mei Ling."* She smiled.

I am Wang Mei Ling.

Then the woman talked to Peter, and soon Peter was smiling, too.

"Yes, Cece, she knows who you are. Your orphanage name was Bei Ma Hua. But they always called you Ying-Ying. It means firefly. You have the same bright eyes. The same mark on your face. She says she would not forget you. She raised you since you were weeks old."

Cece was stunned from the news. *She knows me.*

The woman reached out, her fingertips grazing Cece's cheek. *"Zhen piao liang."*

Cece's face warmed from her touch, bringing her a sense of calm. *Piao liang.* "Pretty. She said I was pretty."

Peter nodded.

Cece studied the woman, and as she looked longer into the woman's eyes, she felt something. Something familiar. Like she had seen that tender expression before. Was she finally connecting with someone at last?

Mei Ling pulled Cece to a nearby sofa, and all of them sat. She shared stories of Cece as a child, and Peter translated.

"You were such a picky eater," Peter relayed. "You did not like to try anything new. Except for ice cream."

Cece smiled.

"You also loved to sing, and you were always very shy about it. But it never took long before you were the loudest of the bunch."

Mei Ling laughed, then she hummed a little tune. It was catchy and melodic.

"That was your favorite song," Peter explained. "It is a popular children's nursery rhyme."

Cece knew then she really was getting a part of her life back and in a way she hadn't expected at all. She thought a simple tour of her own orphanage would have been it. But to meet her own care worker? What luck!

Mei Ling continued on with more stories. How Cece always clung to her leg in front of strangers. How studious she was when she played with her favorite toys. How big hearted when it came to sharing with others. What a sweet child she had been—a joy to love. Then Mei Ling wanted to know everything about Cece. How were her parents? Did she have a nice home? Was she doing well in school? Cece tried to tell Mei Ling everything she could. But soon it was time for Cece to go. One of Mei Ling's children was crying out to her.

Mei Ling had one last thing to say. Her voice became quiet—so quiet Cece could barely hear her.

"What did she say?" Cece asked Peter.

"She says she knows why you came here. Any daughter would want to know. She is not sure if this will help, but she will try."

Then the woman got up and went to a counter. She wrote something on a notepad, then tucked the note into Peter's hand. She shared a few words with him.

Peter said, "We need to go now. We are not to say anything more."

Cece looked quizzically at Peter as her heart drummed in her chest. What had the woman written?

Cece gave Mei Ling a hug good-bye, and Mei Ling whispered in her ear. *"Bu yao ku, baobei."* She pulled away from her and dabbed at the corner of her eye.

When Peter and Cece exited the orphanage, Cece repeated back what Mei Ling had said. *"Bu yao ku, baobei.* Don't…don't what, Peter? Why did she look so sad?"

"She said, 'Don't cry, Cece. That is all.'"

"Don't cry? What did she give you then? What did she tell you in the note?"

"It's an address," Peter said when they reached the elevator.

"An address? For my parents?"

"I don't know, Cece." Peter consulted his map as they stepped into the elevator. "It's not very far." He checked his watch. "But we do not have much time."

They hailed the first cab they saw and soon found themselves in a residential neighborhood made up of rich homes that had sloping gray-tiled roofs and private courtyards. Every dwelling looked meticulously cared for. The streets were swept clean, and the people looked better dressed than the average citizen. Cece filled with consternation. "I don't like this."

The taxi slowed to a stop and parked in front of an impeccable home. It, too, was built in a traditional style, with a sloping gray roof. The front was fenced in with iron and partially obscured by a wooden gate. Cece could make out a fountain beyond the fence and a uniformed attendant working on the landscaping. A brand-new Mercedes was parked along the walk.

What does this place have to do with me? Cece thought.

Everything about it felt wrong. Whoever lived here had money. Lots of it.

Then she saw a boy come out of the house, bouncing a basketball along the walk.

A boy.

Perhaps he was a few years younger, but the sight of him overwhelmed Cece. Was he her replacement? Was he the one who would carry on the family name? Suddenly, her throat felt tight. She could barely find her words. "I can't do this, Peter." Her hands shook in her lap.

Mei Ling had told her not to cry.

"Peter," Cece said louder. "I can't do this."

"But—"

"Don't," Cece said.

Peter didn't say anything. He merely placed a hand over hers, then asked the driver to keep going.

Back at the hotel, Cece was sitting on her bed, her knees pulled up to her chin. Kallyn paced the room. "Cece, you can't draw conclusions like that. You don't even know if that was your parents' house."

Peter nodded from his chair beside Cece's bed. "Kallyn is right. Maybe the people who live there know where they might be."

"I doubt it," Cece said. "Mei Ling told me not to cry." She picked at a loose thread on her shorts. "She knows my story isn't good."

He sighed. "Cece, you could be very wrong."

"Peter, I can put two and two together." She snapped the thread. "I saw the house. I saw the boy. I saw all those girls at the orphanage—"

"You're only guessing," Kallyn said.

Cece's mind couldn't be changed. "Maybe I'm better off not knowing anything."

"Cece," Kallyn said. "I think you're losing sight of the big picture here."

"And that is?"

"You got to meet your care worker, didn't you? Isn't that something? To know what you were like as a child?"

"Yeah, but—"

"You shouldn't let what you saw at that house take that away from you."

"Yes, Cece," Peter said. "You must concentrate on the good."

As Cece looked at her friends, it became clear to her that they didn't understand. She let out a long breath.

Kallyn sat on the edge of her bed. "I'm sure you'll think about this differently if you give it some time."

"I don't think so," Cece said. "Guys, I know you're trying to make me feel better. But let's drop this, okay?"

"Cece," Kallyn said.

"No, I mean it. I want to let it go."

That evening, as Cece rode the overnight train back to Xi'an, she couldn't sleep. Even though she had wanted to let it go, all she could think about was that house in Beijing and that *boy*. She closed her eyes, but the tears still managed to escape.

For so long, she had wanted to believe something that was unlikely to be true, and now the answer seemed to be right in front of her. All those girls in the orphanage— abandoned because of their gender.

It made her question the kind of birth parents she had—what they were capable of. And worst of all, it made her believe she never wanted to know them.

Cece's chest panged with hurt. She turned on her side and pulled the blankets up to her chin. As the train rolled forward, she lay awake, knowing that she couldn't lie to herself anymore.

When the group returned to the dorms the next morning, Cece was exhausted. But there was one thing she had to do. She got out her calling card and dialed the phone in the hall. As the phone rang her house, she tried to breathe evenly.

"Mom?" Cece said.

"Sweetie, is that you? Are you safe in Xi'an now?"

Hearing her mother's voice brought Cece the comfort she longed for. Immediately, her body began to relax. "Yeah, I am."

"Is everything okay?" her mom said.

"I just wanted to tell you I miss you."

"I miss you, too, honey."

Then neither of them said anything.

Finally, her mom spoke. "Cece, you know I love you, right? More than anything."

"I know, Mom." Cece wiped a tear away. "That's why I called."

Chapter Twelve

To: alisofine@e-mail.com
From: cece2me@e-mail.com
Subject: Update...

Hey Al,

I went to the orphanage, and it didn't go as well as I'd hoped. I mean, it did in some ways, and then it really didn't. Don't really want to talk about it. But I will say, why was I in denial for so long?

Cece

To: cece2me@e-mail.com
From: alisofine@e-mail.com
Subject: Re: Update...

Oh, C! Are you okay? Please tell me you're okay. I know you don't want to discuss it now, but I'm here. ((((((Hugs)))))
   I can't wait until you come back home!
   Love,
   A

Monday, Cece's day crawled. She was so tired from the weekend, all she wanted to do was sleep, even though everyone else was worried about midterms that week. She sat through classes in a daze, and, despite herself, her mind constantly drifted back to the weekend. After classes, Cece returned to her dorm. When she walked in, she set her things down and noticed a note on the floor near the door. She picked it up and opened it.

How did everything go?   —Will

Cece sighed. Though she would have liked to have seen Will, she wasn't in any shape to relive Beijing. She slipped the note in her desk drawer and was about to take a nap, when Jess strolled in and laid a bunch of bags on her bed.

"What are you doing here?" Cece said.

"Uh, it's my room, too, remember?" Jessica replied. "Spread out your arms."

"Huh? Why?"

"I'm working on our costumes. I've got to measure you."

"Wait a second…" Cece blinked. "You're *making* our costumes? Why not just get some things from the theater?"

"What would be the point of that when I can design something more beautiful on my own? Now spread 'em."

Cece put her arms out.

Jessica pulled a measuring tape from her handbag and got to work. She wrote down the figures in a little notepad.

Then she emptied a few of her bags and held up some large swatches of fabric. "What color do you want? Keep in mind you're playing a guy. No girly colors."

"Um… blue?"

"Got it. Hey, I already finished the outfit for the concubine. Check it out." She reached into a dress bag and pulled out an elaborate traditional-style gown in gold. She hung it up in her closet. "Lisa's room is packed, so I'm going to keep this here, okay? Don't let anyone touch it."

Cece examined the dress. The details were amazing. "All right, Jess. I didn't say anything before, but now I *have* to know. Where did you learn how to do this?"

"Oh, I've been sewing since I was twelve. My parents think it's just a hobby. But I wouldn't call this a hobby,

would you?" She pointed to the silk embroidery on the bodice of the dress.

"Definitely not."

"Anyway, I told you our costumes would rock." She whipped out a sketch pad from another bag. "See?"

Cece studied Jessica's drawings. One of the sketches was the concubine's outfit. Sure enough the real product looked exactly like the sketch. Jessica had designed a costume for all of the characters in their script.

"The outfits look so authentic," Cece said.

"That's because they are," Jess said. "I went to the Shaanxi Museum and got pictures of what people wore during Qin Shi Huang's time. Once I had that, all I needed to do was sketch them and make up a bunch of patterns. I even borrowed a sewing machine from the school."

"When did you have time to do all this?" Cece said.

"I don't spend every night partying, you know." Jessica put away the fabrics. "Now I just need to get some measurements from Will and Alex." She carried her supplies out the door. "See ya!"

After her roommate left, Cece studied the dress.

Jessica really was a hard person to figure out.

The next couple of days, almost everyone in the program kept it low key, hunkering down to prepare for midterm exams. Cece was glad for the distraction. Maybe it would help her forget about her awful weekend. She met with Peter and Kallyn a couple of times to study, but

188

on one condition—nobody could mention Beijing. Yet by Friday, midterms had come and gone, and Cece still hadn't gotten over what had happened. The prospect of seeing Will that afternoon during her team meeting didn't help either. Surely he would try to bring it up.

Cece went to the theater, and as her team discussed the project, she did her best to avoid looking directly at Will. Alex asked everyone for their progress. Cece reported she was halfway done translating the script. Will gave his ideas about the set, and Alex and Chris discussed the shots they'd be taking. The only question mark was the status on the costumes. Jessica had missed the meeting for some reason, but Chris assured everyone she was making good progress. They'd regroup again next week to begin filming.

After the meeting, Alex started talking to Will about something, and Cece booked it out of the theater. But she hadn't gotten more than ten feet outside of the building when she heard Will calling after her.

"Hey, Cece!"

She turned around and tried to look cheerful. Will caught up with her.

"You seemed so quiet in there, and I haven't seen you around all week. Is everything okay?"

"Yeah, I'm fine."

"Fine?" Will stared at her. "You don't sound fine to me. It's about Beijing, isn't it?"

Cece let out a long breath. *"Well..."*

"Never mind," Will said quickly. "You don't have to talk about it now if you don't want to."

Cece glanced at him. "I don't?"

"No, I can wait. It's all right."

Cece felt relieved. "Thanks, Will," She looked in the direction of her dorm. "So I'll see you later then?"

"Yeah." He slowed down. "Later. But not too much later, okay?" He came to a stop.

Cece nodded. "Okay."

Saturday evening, Cece sat in her room in front of her notebook. It was time to choose a topic for her final paper for Professor Hu's culture class. Cece didn't spend much time debating it. After her recent experience, she had plenty to draw from. She picked up her pen and wrote down her idea: How Backward Thinking Leaves Baby Girls on the Street.

She stared at her words, then crossed them out. Professor Hu probably wouldn't go for that. No instead she'd try... Government Policy and Family Ideals: How the One-Child Policy Orphan's China's Girls.

Good. Cece set down her pen. *Doable.*

Someone knocked. "Cece, it's me," Kallyn said.

Cece got up and opened the door.

"Hey, Kallyn."

She stepped in and sat on Cece's bed. "You know, Cece, you can't spend the rest of the program in your room."

"I wasn't planning to," Cece said. Well, not exactly.

"Yeah, right. Come on. Let's do something fun tonight."

"Like what?"

"Peter mentioned there's a water-fountain show by some pagoda in the city tonight. He says we can't miss it. It's supposed to be absolutely amazing."

"Peter?" Cece said. "Is he here?"

"He might be around," Kallyn replied.

Just then, there was a knock at the door.

When Cece opened it, she saw Peter standing there. "Are you ready to go, Cece?"

But before she could answer, he took one look at her, from her socked feet to her ratty tank top, and said, "Oh, maybe not." He shut the door.

Cece frowned. "What was that all about?"

"We're trying to get you out. Isn't it obvious?" Kallyn stood up and went to Cece's dresser. She pulled out a pair of jeans and a red top. "Put this on." She tossed the clothes at Cece. "Oh, and do something about your hair. Will's waiting in the lobby."

"Will?" Cece stared at her friend. "You invited *Will*?"

"Sorta. He found me and asked if I was hanging with you tonight."

"But Kallyn, I'm hardly in the mood for a night out, especially with Will."

"So?" Kallyn said. "It's not like I'm asking you to take off for Italy or anything. Let's all just hang out a little."

"But—"

"No buts, Cece. You're going out, and we're waiting. Now hurry." She left the room.

Cece stood there for a moment with the top and jeans in her hands. Then she pulled off her clothes and put the outfit on.

Will, Cece, Kallyn, and Peter piled into a cab and headed to Da Yen Ta, the Big Wild Goose Pagoda. On the way, Peter briefly explained what the pagoda was used for. "It was built long ago to hold ancient Buddhist scripts. But now most of us go there for fun. You will see why when we get there."

Half an hour later, the taxi arrived and Cece stepped out of the car. Instantly, she knew she wouldn't regret the evening. A seven-story pagoda stood in the distance, beautifully lit up against the night. A wide, terraced plaza stretched before it, and everywhere, people relaxed, took pictures, and enjoyed the scenery.

"Pretty cool, isn't it?" Will said, standing beside her.

"Yeah," Cece agreed.

Peter glanced at his watch. "We still have twenty minutes before the show starts. I want to show you the pagoda's gardens." He led the way, and Kallyn walked beside him.

"Well, shall we?" Will crooked his arm.

"Um, sure." Cece slipped her arm through his, and they

followed Peter and Kallyn along the edge of the plaza. They entered a landscaped area with winding paths and small hills covered with rocks and greenery.

Cece looked up at the manicured trees. Many of them were lit by spotlights from below, and it was so quiet, she felt like she and her friends were the only ones around. Eventually, Kallyn and Peter pulled farther ahead, or perhaps Will was making them lag behind.

Then suddenly both of them spoke at once.

"Cece…"

"Will…"

"Why don't you start?" Will said.

"Okay." Cece took a deep breath. "I wanted to say I was sorry I couldn't talk to you yesterday."

"That's all right—"

"No, it's not. I know you were only trying to be helpful. It's just…things have been so weird lately."

"So are you ready to talk about it?" Will asked.

"I think so, but what did *you* want to say?" They crossed over a wooden bridge. "I want to hear that first."

"All right. I've finally got some news."

Cece looked up at him. "About your parents?"

"Yeah. Dad dropped the bomb on my mom last weekend."

Cece cringed. "He did?"

"Yeah, and Mom called me at the hotel in Beijing. The conversation did not go well." He stopped to peer at a

gazebo set on a rocky hill among the trees. "She wanted me to come home and talk to my father."

"Oh, Will..."

"But I know Dad's not going to change his mind. Of course, Mom didn't want to hear that coming from me. She totally broke down on the phone."

"That's awful."

"Yeah, well, what else could I do? I think all of us need to face reality, you know?"

"I do," Cece said, thinking of her own circumstances. "But it's not so much fun, is it?"

"Hardly," Will said. "Anyway..." He looked at the gazebo again. "You want to go up there?"

"Sure."

Will stepped onto a boulder and put out his hand. "Come on."

Cece let him steady her as he pulled her up. They picked their way through the rocks until they reached the gazebo. Under the canopy, it was almost completely dark, save for the nearby lights that shined upon the trees. Will leaned over the railing. "So now it's your turn."

Cece placed her hands on the railing. "All right..."

She recounted the entire trip to Beijing, from discovering her orphanage had been torn down to seeing the fancy house with the Mercedes. When she was done, she expected Will to say exactly what Kallyn and Peter had, but he didn't. Instead, he said only, "I'm sorry, Cece. I wish there was something I could do."

"Thanks," Cece said.

"Are you going to go back to the house to find out for sure?"

"No way." The very idea made her sick all over again. "I just wish I could understand it. It's so frustrating to me. How could a mother and father ever think that boys were more valuable than girls?"

"It's a different culture, Cece. I mean, my mom has told me things about China that all sound strange to me. Women binding feet. Men with first, second, and third wives. Of course that's all in the past, but it's part of this country's history. It's almost like asking, Why do Chinese people drink tea?"

Cece thought it over. "True. But it's strange to think that people believe in it so much that they could let their own daughters go."

"I know. It sounds harsh, doesn't it?"

"Completely."

"I guess I don't understand it, either," Will said.

Cece took in a deep breath. "Let's stop talking about this now. It just gets me angry." She straightened. "I want to move on."

"I hear ya," Will said, looking out at the garden below. "Sometimes that's easier."

"Yeah."

"Well, if you change your mind about going back—"

"I don't think I will."

"Hey, guys!" Kallyn called.

Cece peered down and saw her friend waving.

"Peter said the show is about to start," Kallyn said.

"Anyway..." Will said as he helped Cece get down from the gazebo. "I'm glad you came out tonight."

Cece smiled. "*I'm* glad you asked Kallyn to get me out."

Will hopped down to the path. "You are?" He held out a hand for Cece.

"Yeah." She grabbed his hand and jumped down.

He grinned. "Now let's see what this show is all about."

They caught up to Peter and Kallyn, and Peter led them back to the plaza. "To view the show from the right place, we will need to stand in the middle."

Cece looked at the plaza, a long series of wide steps that led to the pagoda. Each step was lit up in a different color by lights that were set flush into the concrete. "I don't get it. Shouldn't we be near a fountain of some kind?"

"Come on, Cece," Will said. "I think I know what's going on."

He pulled her toward the center, following Peter and Kallyn.

When they got to the middle, Will let Cece go and gestured toward the ground. "Look at the steps, Cece. You see all the lights?"

"Yeah."

"I bet the water shoots up from all of those."

Cece glanced behind her, then to the sides. The lights were everywhere. "Oh, no way."

A lady's voice rang out over the loudspeakers. Several people, some with umbrellas, ran out to the plaza and stood on the steps, while spectators gathered around the sides.

"Ready?" Peter said, glancing back at Cece and Will.

Will grabbed Cece's hand. "Don't move."

Cece stiffened. "I can't do this."

Just then, classical Chinese music came on, and water shot up from the steps all around them. Cece squeezed her eyes shut, certain she'd get soaked, but all she could feel was a light mist cooling her face.

"Cece, *look*," Will said.

She opened her eyes. Streams of water swayed all around her, creating beautiful colored arches. The colors and the patterns of the water changed according to the music. Her breath left her.

"So, what do you think?" Will said.

"I think it's the most beautiful thing I've ever seen."

Will looked down at Cece and smiled. "I think it is, too."

Chapter Thirteen

Over the next several days, Cece began putting Beijing behind her, and she was finally able to focus on having a little more fun. Wednesday offered the perfect opportunity when midterm grades came back. Cece, Kallyn, Will, and Peter had all done well, and they were eager to celebrate with a night out. Peter suggested they go to a popular cultural theater show near the city center.

As Cece headed back to her dorm to get ready, she felt better than she had in days, but when she got to her floor, the sight of Jessica bickering on the phone threatened to ruin her mood.

"It was *your* idea to send me here in the first place."

Cece walked toward her room, knowing it had to be Jess's father on the line. Cece got out her key and took her time opening the door.

"No, I'm not going to do that.... I said, 'I'm done.'" Jess sighed loudly. "Fine. See if I care." She hung up.

"What was that all about?" Cece said.

Jessica turned and rolled her eyes. "It's just my parents again." She joined Cece at the door.

"What's going on?"

"I didn't do so hot on my midterms, and Dad's totally flipping out. That's all."

"What do you mean by 'not so hot'?"

"Let's just say that I didn't work too hard at passing. My parents will have to live with the fact that I'm not a budding anthropologist."

The phone rang. Jessica glanced over but she made no move to pick it up. "Don't get that. It has to be my father. Anyway, Cece, don't worry about me. Chris and I are going to a movie tonight with Lisa and Dreyfuss. My midterms will be all but forgotten."

"But don't you think—"

Jessica cut her off. *"Don't worry about it."*

"All right..." Cece bit her lip as she watched Jess go.

Cece met up with Will, Kallyn, and Peter, but she couldn't put Jess out of her mind. On the cab ride to the theater,

Cece filled them in on everything that had happened.

"And her failing midterms surprises you?" Will said. "Jess's idea of studying is figuring out which club to hit next."

"I know, but something doesn't make sense. Have you seen the costumes she's making for our project? They're amazing. Why would she go to all that trouble if she's just going to fail her classes?"

"She's probably just trying to prove something to her parents," Will replied. "She talked about her father all the time, how he had all these hopes for her, and how she felt like such a failure because of it."

"Whatever it is, don't get pulled into this, Cece," Kallyn added. "Let Lisa and Chris cheer her up."

"I agree," Peter said. "It sounds like this is not your problem."

"All right, guys." Cece supposed her friends were right. But she had a feeling that if something didn't change, Jess's situation would only get worse.

When the cab arrived at the theater, Will helped her out of the car and onto the red-carpeted walkway. Cece took in the glamour of the Tang Dynasty Theater. Hostesses opened a pair of giant doors and welcomed them.

"The Tang Theater is Xi'an's premiere cultural show," Peter explained as they waited for an usher to seat them. "It only performs music and dance according to the traditions of the Tang dynasty."

"So what's the big deal about the Tang dynasty?" Will asked.

"It was China's Golden Age. During that time, China was prosperous and culture and music flourished."

"Sorta like the Italian Renaissance?" Kallyn said.

Peter nodded.

An usher led them to their seats in the opulent theater. He directed them to a table toward the front, and Cece could feel the excitement build within her as she took a seat. Not long after, the audience settled down and the lights dimmed.

For the next couple of hours, Cece watched an impressive display of color, sound, and movement. Powerful warriors stomped across the stage wearing frightful masks. Beautiful women with sleeves a mile long created whimsical shapes in the air as they moved to the music. Cece glanced over at Will, who seemed as intrigued as she was. Neither of them said a word. As the show continued, Cece could only think that it was nice to be here. With her friends. Next to Will. It was great to feel good again.

The next day, at the end of culture class, Kallyn and Cece handed in their topics to Professor Hu. The professor peered over her glasses and reviewed Kallyn's first.

"Ah," she said to Kallyn. "I look forward to hear more about uh...Chinese wedding ceremonies."

Kallyn smiled.

Next Professor Hu read Cece's. "Yes," she said, nodding. "This is interesting topic.... I ask you something."

"Okay." Cece said.

"Why you choose this one?"

"Well..." Cece averted her gaze. "It's highly relevant to my circumstances."

"I see." The professor turned the paper over and laid it on her desk. "I give you some advice: Make certain it is not *too* close to you."

"What do you mean?" Cece said.

"An anthropologist must be...how you say...objective?" Cece nodded. "Of course." She could be objective.

"Very well." Professor Hu waved her away. "You may go."

Kallyn and Cece left the classroom. "What was that all about?" Kallyn said.

Cece shrugged. "Beats the heck out of me."

The next two weeks, Cece had to work overtime to keep up with her classes, her team project, and Peter's film-school essays, which she had nearly forgotten about. She also spent more time with Will, Alex, and Chris in the theater, planning and rehearsing shots for their documentary. Jessica was notably missing from most of their meetings, and Chris had to make excuses for her. "Don't worry, guys," he said when Jess hadn't shown up for the *fourth* time. "She's almost done with the costumes, I swear."

"That's not the problem," Alex replied. "She has to participate in this part, too, or we all get penalized."

202

"Who's going to know?" Chris replied.

Alex raised his eyebrows. "If Jess isn't in any of the shots, won't it be obvious?"

"I'm sure she plans to play her role in the film, too. She's just the concubine."

Cece could tell by the way Chris was acting, he wasn't sure at all. She frowned. She was getting irritated with Jess. It was one thing to do the program her way, it was another to affect everyone else.

"We can't mess around anymore," Will said. "We have only a couple of weeks left, and we need to start filming. Someone should talk to her...."

"Or," Alex said, "we could let Mark and Jenny know. I'm not going to lose a college rec because Jess has a hair appointment or something."

"I'll talk to her," Cece said, thinking of what Jess's parents might do to her if she got in serious trouble. "Maybe she'll listen to me."

Will looked at Cece. "You sure?"

"Yeah. I mean, she's my roommate, right? I'll talk to her the next time I see her."

But before she could find Jessica, she had planned to meet up with Peter over lunch. They were going to put the final touches on Peter's film-school essays at the noodle shop. When Cece sat down, though, Peter seemed to have other things on his mind.

He pushed a large manila envelope across the table.

"It's from the director at the orphanage."

Cece paused, feeling her throat dry up.

"Open it, Cece."

She shook her head. "No, you, Peter. It's probably all in Chinese anyway."

"Are you sure?" Peter said.

She nodded.

Peter slowly opened the envelope and pulled out a couple of documents. He scanned the first sheet. "The director writes that she is including your finding record. She has also identified your care worker. If you would like to meet Wang Mei Ling, that can be arranged. She says she hopes the information finds you well...."

Peter flipped the page. "Here is the finding record...."

He scanned the text. "You were found at seven thirty in the morning. You were placed in a cardboard box, and the box was set in front of the orphanage. You were only two weeks old. An envelope was pinned to your blanket. It contained ten yuan and a note stating your birth date. Also in the box were a bottle, a pacifier, and a small toy."

Cece couldn't say anything. Hearing the details of how she had been abandoned felt like someone was poking holes in her heart. What had it been like for her parents to leave her behind at the orphanage? Were they sad? Remorseful? *Did they even look back?*

Peter glanced up. "Are you okay, Cece?"

Cece swallowed. "Yeah, I'm fine." She took the documents from Peter and returned them to the envelope. "That was great. Now why don't we finish your application?"

Peter frowned. "You did not think that was good?"

"What was good?"

"The information about what your parents had given you."

"What about it, Peter? So my parents left me with a few things when they dropped me off. Clearly they didn't need them anymore."

"So you don't think that shows their concern for you?"

Cece sighed. "Well, maybe, but they certainly weren't concerned enough to keep me."

"Cece, your parents left you with only ten yuan. If they lived in the house in Beijing, don't you think they would leave you more?"

She stopped for a second to consider Peter's question. "That doesn't mean anything. They could have been poor when they had me. Or maybe they wanted people to think that whoever left me was poor so they wouldn't be suspected of anything."

"I don't think so," Peter said. "You need to go back to Beijing. Someone in the house must know something. Maybe they can tell you what really happened."

"Go back?" Cece repeated. She grasped for excuses. "But the program is nearly over."

Peter raised an eyebrow. "There is still one free weekend left."

"But what if I don't learn anything new?"

"Then you are no worse off than you were before."

Cece sighed. "I'll think about it."

As night fell, Cece walked back to the dorm, thoughts of Beijing spinning in her mind. A part of her dreaded the idea of returning to that house—and another part of her thought Peter might be right. Then she pictured that boy she had seen at the house, and all of the girls she'd seen in the orphanage. Parents giving up their daughters to have sons. Cece kicked at a rock in her path. It was all too much to deal with. By the time she got to her dorm, she was settled on forgetting Beijing. She'd pretend like she'd never gotten the director's envelope. Erase her conversation with Peter. It was simple. She'd just have to get through the next two weeks, then she could go home and be half a world away.

When Cece got to her room, she dropped her things and glanced at her watch. It was almost eight. She wondered if she should find Jess to talk about their team project, but after a day like this, Jess could certainly wait until tomorrow.

Cece left her room and met Kallyn in the student lounge for a movie.

Kallyn popped a DVD into the player. "I hope you don't mind a romantic comedy."

Cece sat on the couch, sinking into the cushions. "Sounds great to me."

"So..." Kallyn reached into a bag of shrimp chips on the table. "Peter called and told me about the package from the director."

Cece put her feet up. "Well, that boy moves fast."

"You want to know what I think?"

"I have a feeling you're going to tell me anyway."

"Peter is right. You should go back, Cece. I think you're so close to finding out something amazing." She popped a chip into her mouth.

Cece stared at Kallyn. "The last time you said that, my orphanage was torn down and my care worker led me to a house where my rich birth parents live happily ever after with their precious son. Um, thanks, but no thanks."

"You're unbelievable," Kallyn said. "That's not what happened. You *think* that's what happened. You still want to focus on some preconceived notion in your head?"

"Well, that preconceived notion keeps me sane."

"No, it keeps you from going to that house. You're scared, Cece."

"Scared?" *No, it was more like terrified.*

"But you can't let that fear keep you from finding out the answers to your questions."

"Look, I'm doing fine not knowing, okay? In fact, I just realized how pointless it was to start this whole thing to begin with."

Kallyn sighed. "That's what you've been telling yourself?"

"Can we *please* stop talking about it?"

"All right," Kallyn said. "Have it your way." She turned her attention to the TV and hit play on the remote control.

Cece didn't like arguing with Kallyn about Beijing. But the more her friends pressed her about it, the more she doubted she was making the right move.

Chapter Fourteen

The next morning, as Cece left her dorm to go to class, she spotted Will sitting on a bench nearby as if he'd been waiting for her.

"Hey, Cece. I want to talk to you."

"Don't tell me," Cece said as she went up to him. "Peter's gotten to you, too."

"Peter?" Will said. "Gotten to me about what?"

"Oh, uh, nothing," Cece said.

Will stood up. "Let me walk you to class. I'd like to ask you something."

"Okay," Cece said.

They started in the direction to the academic building.

"So," Will began, "a confidential source tells me your birthday is coming up next Wednesday."

Cece rolled her eyes. "By confidential, do you mean Kallyn?" Cece had mentioned it to her last week in passing.

"Maybe. I was thinking since next week will be crazy with finals, we could celebrate this weekend instead. Are you free?"

Cece thought about her last chance to go to Beijing. "Yeah, I'm free."

"Great. I was thinking we could bike around the City Walls? Mark said it's supposed to look awesome from up there at dusk."

"That sounds terrific. I'll ask Peter and Kallyn."

"Actually, I was hoping it could be just the two of us."

Cece stared at him. "You mean...um...like a date?"

"Yeah." Will looked away. "But if you don't want to—"

"No," Cece blurted, "I'd love to go." She could forget about Beijing and bike the City Walls with Will. Perfect.

"Really?" Will said.

"Yeah," Cece replied. "I can't imagine anything better." And she meant it.

Later that day, as Professor Hu wrapped up culture class, Cece gazed off into space, her mind preoccupied with the idea of an evening out with Will.

"So..." Professor Hu said as she walked around the room. "I take time to look at your drafts"—she handed back papers—"I am very, very pleased with progress. Except for one or two of you."

She dropped Cece's paper onto her desk, snapping Cece out of her daze.

Cece glanced down.

It looked like Professor Hu had bled all over her essay. A note in the corner read, *See me after class.*

Great.

"Everyone, consider comments before you write final draft." The professor returned to the front of the room. "Class over."

Everyone got up, except for Cece.

"Come on," Kallyn said.

Cece shook her head. "Don't wait for me."

"You sure?"

She held up her paper for Kallyn to see.

Kallyn winced. "Right. We'll talk later."

Once everyone left the room, Cece grabbed her backpack and went up to Professor Hu.

"So, you didn't like my paper," Cece said.

Professor Hu frowned. "Topic I like. What's in paper, I not so like."

"Why not?" Cece said. "Everything in there is the truth."

"Really?" She took the paper from Cece and read from it. *"The government's idiocy in instituting a one-child policy*

is a hallmark of its fascist politics." She looked up. "This is truth?"

"Well, isn't it?"

"You tell me, Cece." Professor Hu stared intently at her.

"Okay, okay," Cece admitted. "So I was a little angry when I wrote it."

"That is what I am thinking, too. What I say about anthropology? Tell me."

"I must be objective."

"And is this *objective*?"

Cece took the paper back. "No."

"You try again. Show me what truth is. Then we talk."

"All right," Cece said, defeat in her voice. She put the paper into her bag, even though what she really wanted to do was toss it in the trash.

When Cece got back to her room, Jessica was there, hanging up something in her closet.

Jess turned around. "Just the person I wanted to see."

"Me, too," Cece replied, thinking of the talk she needed to have with her roommate. But before she could say anything, Jess said, "Here, try this on." She pulled out a costume from the closet.

Wow. Cece studied the outfit. It was the one for the role of the emperor's adviser—a mandarin-collared, long-sleeved top in royal blue, an embroidered gold sash that went around the neck, and matching pants with an intricate pattern sewn into the cuffs.

"Jess, this is incredible."

"Come on, Cece, I want to see how it fits."

Cece quickly changed into the costume and noticed that even the inside was lined with satin. Then Jess had her stand in front of the mirror.

The clothing fit perfectly.

"Yes!" Jess smiled. "I was worried I hadn't set in the sleeves right. I hope the stuff for the rest of the team fits this well."

Cece began to relax. It was clear Jessica had no intentions of ditching the team. "Jess, I have to apologize."

"For what?"

"I was worried you were going to flake out on us. Now that these are done, we can start filming. Have you memorized your lines yet?"

The expression on Jess's face changed. "Actually... I won't be part of the film."

"What? Why not?"

Jess pulled the concubine outfit from the closet. "I'm not finishing the program." She laid the dress on her bed.

Cece stared at her. "Excuse me?"

"Come on, Cece. Don't be surprised. You know I failed my midterms. There's no way I'll pass now."

"But I don't understand...." Cece looked at her cos-

tume, then the dress on the bed. "Why did you make these if you knew you weren't completing the program?"

"Cece," Jess said, "would you give me some credit? You'd think I'd let you guys film in street clothes? Or worse, in some nasty used thing from the theater?"

"Well..."

"Okay, don't answer that." Jess smoothed out the wrinkles in the concubine dress. "There *is* a little bit more to this."

"What do you mean?"

"These outfits will be excellent additions for my portfolio."

"Portfolio?"

"Yeah, for design school. They'll show off my range."

"I thought you had to apply to an Ivy League."

"Ha!" Jess said. "Like I could even get in."

Cece was confused. "So your dad is okay with you going into fashion now?"

"Are you kidding me?" Jess said. "He has no idea about those plans, but he'll find out soon enough."

She took out a pair of gold shoes from the closet. "It's time I faced him. Once and for all." She set the shoes on the floor. "I can't be the daughter he wants."

"Jess..."

Jessica closed the door to her wardrobe and leaned against it. "I'm tired of fighting so hard to get a tiny glimmer of approval from my parents, you know? All I hear is how I don't live up to their standards. How I disgrace my whole family."

"But you know that's not true."

"Tell my father that." Jess sighed. "You're so lucky, Cece. Your parents—they don't care about all that. They're just glad they have you, right? And they've probably loved you unconditionally since they got you."

Cece didn't know what to say.

Jess took in a deep breath. "This is so dumb. I can't believe I'm letting myself get worked up over this." She yanked a tissue out of a box on her desk. "I just wish...my father understood *me*, you know?"

Cece nodded.

"Anyway..." Jess straightened. "What matters most is that I know who I am and what I want." She swiped at her eyes with the tissue. "If I can remember that, then no one can hurt me. Including him."

Neither of them spoke for a moment. Then finally, Cece said, "Jess, I'm sorry."

"Don't be." She flipped her hair over her shoulder and forced a smile. "A new pair of shoes and I'll be fine."

Cece smiled.

Jess pulled the concubine dress off her bed. "You can play my part, right?"

"Yeah, I guess."

"Then try this on. I only have tonight to make adjustments. I leave tomorrow."

"*Tomorrow?* So soon?"

"Cece, I held out as long as I could. My father wanted me home when I failed midterms."

"So how did you get him to let you stay?"

"I told him I had to finish what I was doing for you guys, and of course, he couldn't let *his daughter* screw up things for other people. He gave me two weeks, and that ends tomorrow." Jess held up the dress. "Now come on."

Cece got up, then looked right into Jess's eyes. Her roommate looked more determined than ever. Cece took the costume. "Jess?"

"What is it, C?"

"I just wanted to say..." Cece bit her lip, thinking about her situation. How hesitant she was to confront her own problems. How afraid. "Well, I just wanted to say... I wish I had your courage."

Jess smiled. "Thanks, Cece."

Early the next morning, Jessica set her bags by the door, and they said their good-byes.

"E-mail me, okay?" Cece said.

"I will." Jessica hung her purse over her shoulder. "Oh, and before I go... I wanted to wish you luck with Will."

Cece tensed. She wasn't sure if Jess was being sarcastic or serious. "Um...what?" Though it was no secret that she and Will had been hanging out, she didn't think Jess had been around enough to notice.

"Cece, you must think I'm brain-dead," Jess said. "Ever

since I saw you two chatting it up at the club, I knew you liked him, though I didn't want to admit it."

"Really?"

"Who *doesn't* think he's hot, C? And the guy is crazy about you, too. Has been since the beginning. Whenever I was with him, all he did was ask where you were, when you were going to come out with us.... It drove me nuts."

"He did?"

"Yeah. And I guess it would have been nice if I had mentioned that to you, but you know..." She flipped her hair over her shoulder.

"I understand." Though Cece wasn't exactly thrilled that Jess had held out on her, she was glad she had told her. It was reaffirming to know her earlier suspicions about Will had been right.

"Anyway, I had to get that off my chest. Confession time is now up! I better go if I want to get to the airport early. I'm dying to buy some duty-free stuff." She gave Cece a hug.

Someone knocked. "That's gotta be Chris," Jess said. "He's helping me take my things down." She grabbed the handle to one of her suitcases. "I'll keep in touch, Cece. Bye!"

After Jess left, Cece leaned against the door. She was sad to see her roommate go. But as Cece moved away from the door, she smiled.

Jess was going after what she wanted now.

And that was something to be happy about.

That Thursday, Cece was sitting at her desk in her half-empty room. Without Jess's things around, the place looked about as bleak as her culture paper. All she had written was a giant tirade about how Chinese people didn't value girls, with little evidence to back it up. "Show me facts," Professor Hu had written in the margins. "Must have facts."

Cece tried searching for data online. How many girls were abandoned in China prior to the enactment of the one-child policy? How many were abandoned after? She couldn't find hard numbers about female population in Chinese orphanages. She found only a figure for both boys and girls combined. According to China World News, only twenty thousand children were in state care in 2002. *Out of 1.2 billion people?* The number seemed way too low. It didn't make sense.

She tried to see if anyone had done studies on China's orphanages that might support her theory. She came across one report by the Human Rights Watch from 1996. It stated, "The vast majority of children in orphanages are, and consistently have been during the past decade, healthy infant girls; that is, children without serious disabilities who are abandoned because of traditional attitudes that value boy children more highly." But the source of that information was from "anecdotal and journalistic reporting." So was that fact? She didn't think so.

Cece decided to go at the information from another

angle. She wanted to see if there were data that might show a disparity between how women were treated in this country versus men—something that might indicate that girls were indeed less valued than boys. Did women have unequal access to higher education? She looked at enrollment figures for universities and found that almost half of the student population in China was female. *Hmm*... that didn't help. She expected the difference to be enormous. She then looked at labor force statistics. Again, nothing that would suggest women did not have equal opportunities at work.

Annoyed, Cece packed up her laptop, called Peter, and asked to meet him at the café by the university. Maybe he could help her understand why nothing added up.

When she arrived, she connected to Wi-Fi and showed Peter what she'd found.

"It's like there's a conspiracy or something," Cece said. "I can't prove that boys are valued here more than girls."

Peter shrugged. "Maybe it's because there is nothing to prove."

"But there is, Peter," Cece said. "I literally saw with my own two eyes all the girls at that orphanage. Don't you think that speaks for itself?"

"To some extent, it does," he said. "But this is the problem. You are making it sound like almost everyone is giving up girls for boys. I don't think that is true because you just said twenty thousand children out of 1.2 billion."

"Yeah, but that number must be way understated."

"Even if it is," Peter said, "do you believe our country is filled with homeless girls?"

"Well, no. Maybe they were all adopted to other countries. Like me."

"Let's look." Peter typed his search on the Internet. "It says in 2005, about eight thousand Chinese children total were adopted to foreign countries."

"Only eight thousand?"

"So where are the girls you think China abandons all the time?"

"Peter, I don't know." Cece held her head in her hands.

"Maybe you are looking for something that isn't there."

"No, I'm not," Cece said indignantly. Then she felt herself giving in a little. "Okay, so maybe not *everyone* here thinks boys are more important than girls."

"Maybe?"

"Okay, so it's possible I've been generalizing...a little."

"Good," Peter said. "I'm glad you can see it now."

"See what?"

"See why you need to go back to Beijing."

Cece squeezed her eyes shut. *"Peter."*

"Cece, you say you came here to find answers, but now you are trying to go back home with only more questions." He got up. "Think about that." And as if to emphasize his point, Peter just walked out, leaving her to herself.

Cece blew air at her bangs. She was so frustrated. She

thought over what Peter had said about going home with more questions. But it was so much easier to forget what she had learned while she was here. Or was it? Cece played with a napkin on the table. Since Beijing, the image of the house and that boy had entered her mind one too many times. Would she ever really be able to forget?

Cece shut her laptop and packed up. So many thoughts swirled in her head as she went back to her dorm. She thought about how she felt before she left for China—so determined to find out why she had been abandoned. So excited to learn more about where she came from, who her parents were. Then she thought about her time in China— getting to know Jessica and understanding the strictness of her parents; meeting Peter's mother and father, who seemed so different from Jess's family; and finally Will, who hardly seemed any more Chinese than Cece. What was she to learn from all of this?

When she returned to her room and got ready for bed, she contemplated the orphanage. All those girls, their smiling faces. They all had their own stories, didn't they? Like Jess, like Peter, like Will... like her. So why couldn't she just go find out what hers was?

Cece lay in bed, trying to determine the answer, and when she finally found a way to put it in words, every part of her cringed. She knew what the possible consequence of approaching that fancy house in Beijing was. She knew

what could happen if she met her birth mother and father.

She'd already felt rejected by them once. Could she risk being rejected *twice*?

That was it, wasn't it? Her worst fear. Was she strong enough to weather that? Cece glanced at Jess's empty bed. Could she spend her whole life feeling like her birth parents never accepted her, like Jess? What was it that her roommate had said? "If I know who I am and what I want, no one can hurt me."

Was that true?

Cece took out her picture from the orphanage. The girl staring back was still a stranger, even after all this time. And the longing within Cece to know herself burned stronger.

You are trying to go back with only more questions, Peter had said.

She knew then that it wasn't a matter of personal choice. It wasn't a matter of fear anymore.

She got out of bed and pulled out her overnight bag.

Tomorrow evening, she had to go to Beijing.

The next day, before Cece met with her project team, she, Kallyn, and Peter met in her room. She told them about her change of plans.

"Finally," Kallyn said, "Cece listens to the voice of reason."

"It's because I left you at the table, isn't it?" Peter said. "I thought that was a nice touch."

Cece smiled.

"I'll get us train tickets tonight." Peter got up to leave.

"Wait, Peter." Kallyn looked at Cece. "Do you want me to come, too?"

Cece hesitated. "Actually...I'd like to do this on my own, as much as I can. But Peter, I will need you."

"Sure," Peter said.

Kallyn nodded. "I understand. I'll be pulling for you, Cece."

After they broke up, Cece headed to the theater, thinking about how she was going to rearrange her schedule to fit in the trip to Beijing. By the end of today, the team would be about three-quarters done with the shots they needed. They'd already planned to meet Monday and Tuesday to finish. Finals were on Wednesday and Thursday—her culture paper would be due, and she'd have to take massive tests for other classes. Then Friday team projects would be presented. Her last week would be horrendous.

"Hey, Cece!"

Cece turned to see Will running up to her.

"I was thinking that I'd stop by your room around six?"

Her birthday plans. "Will, I'm sorry," Cece said. "I can't go anymore. I was just going to tell you."

Will looked concerned. "What happened?"

"I'm going to Beijing."

A grin spread across his face. "You are?"

"Yeah," Cece said. "I take it you think it's the right move."

Will nodded. "But I knew it had to be your decision. Do you need me to come with you? I'd be happy to."

"No, that's okay. Peter is already going. I'll be fine."

"You sure?"

"Yeah, thanks for the offer."

"Well, all right then. Maybe we'll have something even more to celebrate when you get back."

Cece bit her lip. "I hope so."

That evening, Cece boarded the train with Peter. While Peter stayed in another compartment, Cece lay in her sleeper, watching the shadows of the night flash across the walls. She felt like she was wandering into the big unknown, but mixed in with all the nervousness, she was oddly proud. She really was doing this, and somehow, she knew that Will was right. Everything *was* going to be okay.

When Cece and Peter arrived in Beijing the next morning, they hailed a cab and went directly to the house. The Mercedes was gone, and the yard was empty. "Now don't be nervous," Peter said. "Let me do the talking."

"Easier said than done." Cece rubbed her hands against her jeans and took a few deep breaths.

They got out of the cab and crossed the street. Peter

found a speaker in front of the wooden gate. "I will ask for the master of the house."

"Sure." Cece leaned against the gate, thankful to be leaning against something.

Peter pressed one of the buttons, and the ringer buzzed. A few moments later, a man's voice came on over the speaker. Peter and the man exchanged a few words.

"It is the attendant," Peter whispered to Cece. "He wants to know what we want with the master."

Cece shrugged. "Should we make up something?"

"No," Peter said, "I will just tell him it's important."

"Sounds good to me."

Peter spoke into the speaker again, and the man replied.

"This is not so easy," Peter said. "He wants to know *why* it's important."

"Unbelievable." Cece said. She stared at the gate. *Think, Cece.* "Maybe we should mention that the care worker sent us here?"

"Good. I will do that."

Peter spoke into the speaker once more.

After a momentary pause, Cece heard the man say, *"Wang Mei Ling?"* as if he was surprised. Then he said, *"Deng yi xia."*

Cece knew this one. It meant *wait.* "So he's getting somebody?"

"Maybe," Peter said. "The attendant's coming."

Cece straightened. *This is it.*

The lookhole in the gate opened, and an older man peered at Peter and Cece. Then he conversed with Peter. Cece heard Peter mention the care worker's name again.

Breathe, Cece, breathe. She was starting to feel dizzy.

The man stared intently at Cece. "Bei Ma Hua?"

Peter nodded.

Bei Ma Hua, Cece thought. That was her name at the orphanage. "Peter, he knows me?"

Before Peter could answer, the man opened the gate. *"Wo de tian, ah,"* he said, a serious expression on his face. *"Ni shi lai zhao wo ma?"* His eyes began to brim with tears. *"Ni shi lai zhao wo?"*

Cece looked back at the man. "What's he saying, Peter?"

"He says, 'Have you come to find me?'"

What? Cece glanced from the man to Peter, confused.

The man continued to speak. A tear slid down his cheek. *"Ni shi wo de nuer."*

This time, Cece realized what the man had said as soon as Peter had.

You are my daughter.

Chapter Fifteen

Cece found herself in a long embrace. This man was her father? *But how?* She couldn't move, couldn't speak. Her father pulled back from their hug. Cece searched his face, looking for a resemblance, and now she could see it. His cheeks—they were rounded like hers. His chin, just as sharp.

"Wo jiao Shao Yi Mou," he said.

Shao Yi Mou. Her father's name. She still couldn't believe he was standing right in front of her. Her dad. Her eyes welled with tears. *"Wo, wo jiao Cece,"* she managed to say.

"Cece," her father said perfectly. It was as if the name couldn't have sounded more beautiful to his ears. *"Lai, lai."*

Come. Cece tried to compose herself as he ushered them into the courtyard and toward the back of the house. As Cece walked, her shock quickly turned into anticipation. What would her dad say to her? What would she find out? She looked at Peter, who gave her a reassuring smile. They came to a weathered door, then stepped inside. Cece took in the tiny, barely furnished room. There was only a small cot, a few chairs, and a table. Above the table, some dishes were stacked on a shelf, and in the opposite corner, a shower curtain was drawn across a narrow doorway.

Her father dusted off a couple of the chairs and gestured toward them. *"Zuo."*

Cece and Peter sat down. As Cece nervously played with the edge of her shirt, she studied her father as he warmed a teapot. He was wearing a simple collarless button-down and loose-fitting pants. Almost like pajamas. From the creases of his clothing, she could make out his thin frame. How long had she wondered where she'd gotten her lanky stature? Now she knew.

When her father turned with two mugs brimming with tea, Cece smiled, an effort to appear calm.

He smiled back and handed Peter and Cece the mugs.

Though Cece wasn't thirsty, the cup felt comforting in her hands, and the warmth of the mug stilled her.

Then Yi Mou—or should she call him *Baba?* or Father? she wasn't sure—sat opposite Cece on the cot and started talking to Peter.

Peter said, "He wants to tell the story he has waited so long to tell you."

Cece nodded, eager to listen.

Her father began.

"Twenty years ago," Peter translated, "your father came from the country to find work. It was here in Beijing that he got a job as an attendant for a government official. His wife, An Wei, your mother..."

My mother? Cece immediately wondered where her mom was. It was clear from the room, she didn't live there. Cece looked at her father, but didn't want to interrupt.

"Your mother," Peter said, "was also an attendant at the house. They fell in love and married. The master supported the marriage, but his wife did not. She thought it was shameful to house a family as if they ran a charity."

Cece's father shook his head as he spoke.

"But the master prevailed," Peter translated, "allowing your parents to live in this room so long as their work would not suffer. Of course, your parents wished for a child, and when An Wei became pregnant, they were over-joyed. The official's wife was very upset.

"Your father knew his master's good graces would not last long," Peter continued. "He only hoped he could find

new work so he could keep the family together. But things did not go as planned.

"He couldn't find a better job. He had no education, and no one would take his family in. As An Wei grew larger with child, their worry increased. Yet despite everything, An Wei remained optimistic. Perhaps, she thought, when the official's wife saw the child, she'd be compassionate. She would be unable to put them out."

Yi Mou paused and looked directly at Cece, as if to emphasize his next words.

"This is what your mother hoped for every day," Peter said. "Every night."

Cece nodded, but her body tensed.

"One evening, your father came home from an errand and found An Wei in bed....She was not feeling well. She was certain the baby would be coming soon....The next day, An Wei was still not well. She got up to try to do her master's laundry, and your father insisted she stay in bed. She refused....She would not neglect her duties."

Suddenly, the mug Cece was holding felt very cold.

"All morning she washed clothes outside while Yi Mou completed errands. When he came home, he found An Wei collapsed on the ground."

Cece's heart started to pound.

"At the hospital, the doctors wouldn't let your father see her. They worked on An Wei for hours."

No. Cece's chest tightened even more.

Her father's voice was shaking.

Cece could no longer look at him. She stared at the tea in her hands.

"When the doctors were done," Peter continued, "they brought out a child—a beautiful child."

Her father's voice was now barely a whisper.

"They told Yi Mou that An Wei...that An Wei had passed."

Cece's vision blurred with tears. *"No."*

Peter took her tea from her and tried to hold her hands. "It's okay, Cece."

Her shoulders shook. Her mother was gone. She had wanted to know her so badly. Now it all made sense. Mei Ling's warning. *Don't cry.* But Cece could do nothing to stop herself.

Her father spoke again. This time his voice was calm. *"Ni de mama meiyou zou,"* he said.

Cece wiped at her face and looked at her father. "She's not gone," Peter said.

"Ta yongyuan huo zai ni de xing zhong."

And for whatever reason, Cece understood her father clearly. "She's always lived in my heart," she said.

Her father continued speaking, a warm smile on his face.

"He says he knows it was she who led you to him after all this time."

The tone of her father's voice was certain, matching the

expression in his eyes, and Cece wanted to believe him. She nodded, and he continued the story.

"After Yi Mou lost his wife," Peter said, "he had no time to grieve. He had a hungry child to feed. The master gently told him that China would allow foreign adoption soon and, as healthy and beautiful as you were, it would be certain you would go to a good home."

Her father paused. *"Wo zhidao zhe shi ni de mingyun."*

"Yi Mou knew this was your destiny. He and An Wei had wanted nothing more than for you to be well cared for.... He was determined to fulfill his wife's wishes and his own.... The day he took you to the orphanage, he felt like An Wei had guided him."

The look in Cece's father's eyes grew distant, as if he was imagining himself there, and Cece bit back her tears.

"He felt no pain," Peter said. "No regret. He packed the few things they had for you and all the money he could give in a cardboard box. Then, in the early hours of morning, he left you at the doorstep of the orphanage."

Cece took in a slow breath. How she wished things could have been different. Not for herself, but for her father. Though she knew now he had made the right decision to leave her.

"Wo yizhi zai pangbian deng zhe," he said.

"Your father waited nearby," Peter explained. "It wasn't long before you began to cry, and a care worker came out and found you. The care worker was Wang Mei Ling. She picked you up and carried your belongings inside. Every day, your father hoped the foreign adoption policy would pass in government. His master insisted it would. But for nearly two years, nothing happened. Each day that passed, Yi Mou would go to the orphanage and peek through the gates, hoping to see you. Finally, one fine morning he did."

Cece's father smiled broadly as he spoke. It was obvious how much he cared for her.

"Mei Ling was taking you out for a walk. You were bigger and rounder and more beautiful than ever.

"Each day, he'd return during the same time to see you come out. Eventually, he dared to talk to Mei Ling. He never told her who he was, but he would say how lovely you were and leave Mei Ling a small envelope with his address and some money.

"Mei Ling understood exactly who your father was."

"Ta changchang gei wo xie xing."

"She would write to him often and let him know how you were doing. It was a great day when Mei Ling wrote that the orphanage was accepting adoptions from foreign countries. Many, many children would find new homes. It was only weeks until you had new parents...."

My parents, Cece thought.

Her father clasped his hands together. *"Wo feichang xingfen. "*

"Yi Mou could not have been happier," Peter said. "Mei Ling told him what little she knew about your parents. They were from the United States. They were kind. So excited to have a child at last. Best of all, Mei Ling told him how your new mother had held you for the first time. She pulled you in close and sweetly uttered three Chinese words. *Wo ai ni."*

I love you. Cece felt the tears coming again.

Her father's eyes shined with joy as he spoke.

"And now you have come to find me."

"Ni tongshi ye ba nide muqing dai dao wo de sheng-bian."

"You have also brought a part of my wife to me."

Cece's father reached by his bedside and showed her a photograph.

Cece held the picture of a woman standing beside her father. She recognized her own eyes, her own smile. "An Wei," she said. *"My mother."* A tear ran down her cheek, and something in her heart locked into place.

"Ta feichang ai ni, jiu xiang wo yiyang."

"She loved you as much as I do." Cece stared at her father, and she couldn't hold back any longer. She stood up and hugged him, burying her head into his shoulder. *"Baba..."* she murmured, no longer confused, no longer afraid of the truth.

• • •

That evening, on the way to the train station, Cece sat with Peter in a cab, her mind still buzzing with the memory of meeting her father. She couldn't stop thinking about how things would be different now. Especially at home.

"Are you okay?" Peter said.

"I'm fine," Cece said. "It's just all overwhelming. I'm just wondering how I'm going to tell my parents about all of this."

"Will they be supportive?" Peter asked. "You will see your birth father again, right?"

"I think my dad will be okay with it...but I'm not sure about my mom."

"I am sure she will be happy for you," Peter said.

Cece sighed. He didn't know her mother. "Let's hope so."

When they got to Xi'an the next morning, Cece didn't want to call her parents from the dorm. She needed privacy, so she dropped her things off in her room and found a phone booth just outside the university. Cece pulled out her calling card and punched in the numbers, but as she reached the last digits, she slowed down. How was she going to break the news? Should she start with what she'd just learned or go from the very beginning? Should she tell them everything or only the highlights? *You're overthinking this.* She punched in the last number. *Say whatever comes to you.*

The phone rang as Cece twisted the cord in her hand.

"Hello?"

"Mom?"

"Cece! What a surprise. I figured you'd be too busy with finals to call—"

"Mom, wait—there's something I need to tell you."

Her mom paused. "Is everything all right?"

"Listen, could you get Dad on the phone, too?" Cece leaned against the booth. She heard her mother call for her dad. "Honey," her mom said, "what is it?"

"Everything's fine. I just have some news." Cece closed her eyes. *Big news. News you probably don't want to hear.*

Cece heard her father pick up the line.

"Cece, are you okay?" His tone was serious.

"Yeah."

"What's going on then?"

She took in a breath. She let the words come out on their own. "Well...it's about Beijing...."

She told the story as best she could. From the beginning. The trip to the orphanage. Finding Mei Ling. Then going back again and meeting her father. When she finally finished, there was complete silence on the line.

"Um... Mom, Dad, are you there? Say something."

"I'm here," her father said. "Your mother is...well, she's a little upset."

This was exactly what she was afraid of. "She's not mad, is she?"

"No, give her a few seconds. She's...um...overwhelmed. And I have to admit I am, too."

"I'm sorry, Dad. I didn't mean to—"

"Cece, don't apologize."

Cece shook her head. No, she had to. She knew she'd hurt her mother. "Dad, could you tell Mom...well, could you tell her..."

She heard her mother clear her throat. "I'm right here, honey."

"Mom, I just wanted to say..." Cece pressed a hand against the booth. It was so hard to get it out, but it was something that was long overdue. "You'll always be my mother, you know? Always. That was never going to change."

Her mom didn't respond at first.

Then Cece could hear her weeping softly.

"I don't know why I've never said that to you," Cece continued. "I guess I was sorta angry. Every time I tried to ask about my adoption—"

"Don't say another word," her mother said. "I'm the one who's sorry."

"You? Why?"

"I should have been more open from the beginning, but I was so afraid you'd be hurt. I wanted to protect you even though I didn't know what I was protecting you from."

Cece held the phone tighter. "Oh, Mom."

"I just wish you didn't have to go through this. You're my baby, you know?"

"I know," Cece said. "But I'm okay." She longed to be home with her mother, to hug her, to show her she was all right. "I really am."

Her mother breathed in. "It makes me feel so much better to hear that."

"Mom, there's just one more thing I need to say."

"Yes?"

Cece pictured her mother on the other end of the phone and smiled. *"Wo ai ni."*

That evening, Cece and Will carried out their original plans for Cece's birthday, with one teeny exception. They brought company. Cece couldn't bear to celebrate without Kallyn and Peter. They had so few days left together before it would be time to head home. Peter took them to the Muslim Quarter for an early dinner so Cece could reminisce about the first Chinese meal in China she ever liked, and then they wandered around the area to pick up some last-minute souvenirs. Afterward, they took a lazy bike ride atop the City Walls while the sun began its descent.

When they finished, Will and Peter returned the bikes while Cece and Kallyn looked over the wall, taking in the view. The sky was a mixture of orange and purple, and the Bell Tower and the Drum Tower were lit up, standing out among the buildings below. Cece thought about their first excursion weeks ago.

Kallyn seemed to be thinking about the same thing. "Can you believe it's been over two months since we were last here?"

Cece gazed at the fading sun. "I know."

"In one short week, I'll be home."

"With Ryan," Cece said. "Wait—you two are still together, right? It's been so long since we've talked about him."

Kallyn grinned. "It's okay. You were kind of distracted."

Cece laughed. "Just a little."

"No worries, though. Check this out." She pulled out a necklace that was tucked under her shirt. A tiny key dangled from it. "Ryan sent it to me."

"Let me guess—the key to his heart?"

"Nope, it goes to a lock for my new mountain bike. When I get back, Ryan's taking me on a huge cycling trip through the Rockies." She let out a breath. "I think I'm in love."

"Yeah?"

"Totally." Kallyn glanced past Cece. "Speaking of love..." she whispered.

Will joined Cece's side. "Well, the bikes are turned in."

Peter stood next to Kallyn. "What did I miss?"

"Oh, nothing," Kallyn said. "Cece, Will, you two enjoy the view. Peter, let's go take a walk."

"A walk?" Peter said. "But we just biked for an hour."

Kallyn gave him a funny look. "*Come on*, Peter."

Cece laughed as Kallyn pulled Peter away. "She is hardly subtle, huh?"

Will smiled as he studied the horizon. "Hardly. But I'm glad it's just you and me now."

Cece's heart skipped a beat. "Me, too."

Will grasped the edge of the wall. "And I'm glad things worked out in Beijing, Cece. What you did took some guts." He looked at her. "Makes me wonder if I have that kind of courage."

"What do you mean?"

"I don't know," Will replied. "The courage to go after what I want, I guess. Like my father is. He's officially filed for separation now."

"I'm sorry, Will." Cece touched his arm.

"No, it's all good. It is. It's what I have to learn." He turned to face her. "Maybe I should start now."

Cece tilted her head. "Start what?"

Will took her hand. "Going after what I want."

Cece's voice was barely audible. "Oh?" She stared at his dark eyes, his perfect lips.

"Uh-huh." Will pulled her toward him.

And they kissed like it was a kiss they had waited for all summer long.

Chapter Sixteen

The next couple of days were busier than ever before. No classes were held on Monday or Tuesday, allowing students to prepare for finals on Wednesday. Cece spent her time studying for her exams, meeting with her project team to finish their documentary, and finishing Peter's film-school essays. But she worked hardest of all on her culture paper—a paper she could now tackle with renewed inspiration.

By Thursday, Cece had put her exams and paper behind her; all that was left to do was the team project presentation and one more proofread of Peter's essays. The last

day's schedule would begin with the presentations and fin-ish with an awards ceremony. The students gathered in the lecture hall, and everyone critiqued each team's project. She was pretty impressed with the documentaries, but per-sonally, she thought her team's was the best. Not only were their costumes one of a kind—thanks to Jessica—but their script was accurate *and* humorous. Cece did a decent job playing Qin Shi Huang's male adviser, and at the end of the film, her untimely death as a concubine was a big hit.

After the critiques came in and the scores were tabu-lated, Mark and Jenny went up to the podium to award final points. Cece's team received full marks. "And," Mark said, "we're going to play *Qin Shi Huang: One Man, One Country* next year as the leading example. Team Three, please stand."

Cece's team got to their feet, and the audience cheered. It was nice to get credit for their hard work.

After the clapping subsided, the professors presented awards, citing who would receive college recommenda-tions. As each professor took his turn, Alex's name kept coming up. Cece was psyched when she and Kallyn both received recs for archaeology and evolution. Finally, it was Professor Hu's turn to announce her list. Cece held her breath. She knew she'd taken a risk with her paper, but at the same time, she thought she turned in something great. Her nervousness got worse when Professor Hu slowly and methodically named her top students. Instead of just say-

242

ing the names, she expanded upon them, citing the reasons why she had selected each one.

"And...Jeremiah, he also do very well," she said. "I very much enjoy his paper on feng shui and Chinese architecture. I think his analysis of home design was very interesting—earth, water, wind, fire...."

Cece's knee began to bounce. A couple of people coughed.

"However, the student whose essay I appreciate most, putting her at top of class"—she peered down at the paper she was holding—"is...Cece Charles for 'Government Policy and Family Ideals: How the One-Child Policy Affects China's Orphans.'"

Cece grinned.

"In this essay, Cece separates fact from fiction. Truth from assumption. Objectivity from bias." Professor Hu pointed at the paper. "And this is my favorite line: 'One must not look for answers that fit the observation, but ask the questions that arise from the observation. Only then will the truth reveal itself.' And then she also say... 'Because abandonment is illegal, there is little data to measure,' therefore...conclusions must draw from anecdotal evidence, and *that*"—she took in a huge breath—"is the truth. I think she say this like real anthropologist. It is very, very good, yes?"

At first no one clapped, but soon the auditorium filled with applause.

Cece listened to the praise and swallowed. Will gave her a smile.

Maybe the truth didn't always have to hurt.

The next day, students started leaving for their flights. Because everyone was departing at different times, most of the students arranged for their own transportation. Cece, Will, Peter, and Kallyn headed to the airport together. Peter saw them off outside the terminal, and after saying goodbye to Will and Kallyn, he gave Cece a hug.

"I will miss you, Xiao Mei."

"Thank you so much, Peter," Cece said. "I couldn't have done it without you."

He let her go. "Anytime you need to find a missing relative, you talk to Da Ge, okay?"

Cece laughed, then reached into her bag. She handed him a manila envelope.

"What is this?" Peter studied the package.

"Open it, but be careful."

Peter pulled out his finished film-school application. "I thought you forgot this a long time ago."

"I guess I had *not* forgotten." Cece smiled.

He smiled back, and they hugged one more time. "Write me, okay?"

Cece nodded.

Then Peter walked back to the cab, turned, and pointed at Cece. "I'll see you in L.A., baby."

After he left, Will put an arm around her. "Hard to see him go, huh?"

"Yeah," Cece said as she watched the taxi pull away.

They all went inside, then scanned the departure boards. Cece's flight was departing on time. She had hoped her plane would be delayed so she wouldn't be the first to leave. She just wanted a little more time with her friends.

Will helped her check in, and she had to say good-bye.

Cece gave Kallyn a hug. "Thanks for everything."

"You're welcome," Kallyn said. "Maybe I'll see you at Christmas? My grandma lives in Fort Worth. I think it's her turn to host the Sullivans this year."

"That would be great."

"So this isn't a good-bye, it's a 'see you later,' okay?"

Cece grinned. "Right. Until Christmas, then."

Will and Cece looked at each other, and Kallyn, ever the sensitive friend, started walking toward a gift shop.

Now it was just the two of them.

"This is it, I guess," Will said.

"Yeah…" There were so many things Cece knew she should say to him about where they stood and what would happen from here, but the last few days all she had done was avoid the subject. She only wanted to enjoy every second she had with him. But now, they would have to get things clear. Cece opened her mouth, uncertain how to begin. "Will, I…well…I…" She had no idea how to start.

Will laughed. "Cece, you don't have to say anything."

"I don't?"

"No, we should do what we want, right?"

"What do you mean?"

"Well, if you want to call me, then call me. Let's do whatever comes naturally, okay? We shouldn't force anything."

Cece let out a breath. It was like Will was saying exactly what she was thinking. "That sounds perfect."

"So we better get started."

"Doing what?"

Will lifted her chin. "Whatever comes naturally." He leaned in for a kiss.

Cece melted into his arms, determined to remember the moment forever.

After they said their good-byes, Cece walked to her gate. All around her people bustled by, headed for their flights. As Cece passed the restaurants and the shops, she remembered how she had felt when she first arrived in China. Nervous. Intrigued. Eager to know more. She had been a girl looking for answers to her past. But now, as she began her journey home, she was a girl who couldn't wait to discover her future.